"I never mentioned love to you. Did I?"

Melissa shook her head.

"Did your *friend* from before tell you he loved you?" Bret asked.

Blinking back sudden tears, Melissa nodded.

"So you know there is no dependency in the word. Don't confuse lust for love, Melissa...I want you."

Barbara McMahon, her husband and teenage daughter share their home with one dog and four cats in the San Francisco Bay area. She works for a computer software company, writing on weekends and in the evenings. A love for romances and happy endings led to a strong desire to create stories she'd like to read herself. In earlier days she visited exotic locales when she flew for an international airline, and now she uses some of these places in her books. Her hobbies are reading, skiing and writing.

Books by Barbara McMahon

HARLEQUIN ROMANCE
3369—WANTED: WIFE AND MOTHER

Look out in October 1996 for Barbara McMahon's next book, *Wyoming Wedding* (#3428), which has been warmly received by the critics.

"McMahon brings vivid characters to life that will endear themselves to readers, along with clever scenes and ingenious dialogue."

—*Romantic Times*

Shining Through
Barbara McMahon

Harlequin Books

TORONTO • NEW YORK • LONDON
AMSTERDAM • PARIS • SYDNEY • HAMBURG
STOCKHOLM • ATHENS • TOKYO • MILAN
MADRID • WARSAW • BUDAPEST • AUCKLAND

ISBN 0-373-17287-7

SHINING THROUGH

First North American Publication 1996.

CHAPTER ONE

IT WAS glorious! Melissa raised her face to the sun and danced a small step across the verdant meadow, the lush grass warm beneath her bare feet. It was a beautiful day and she planned to enjoy it fully. Twirling around, her arms upraised, she smiled up at the cloudless blue sky in total bliss, revelling in the sun's heat.

Above her the mountains of Austria soared, grey granite peaks still covered with dazzling white snow. Lower on the slopes, lush summer-green meadows were dotted with wild flowers like the flat green meadow she'd discovered exploring yesterday. The nearby woods, edging her own meadow, seemed dark and mysterious contrasted to the open field, the tall pines and firs shading the needle-strewn ground from the sun's kiss. The dense stand of trees isolated the meadow. But the open view across the valley was spectacular. It was wonderful and Melissa drank in the beauty like a thirsty man in a hot desert.

Melissa was so caught up in her own pleasures of the meadow that she didn't notice the man who sat so silently in the shadow of the forest, watching her.

She smiled again in her delight and feasted her eyes on the view, studying each detail. To the left she saw the old stone buildings of Salzburg shimmering in the summer sun, their edges blunted with distance, the patina of the years enhancing their rich baroque beauty. The many church spires looked like drizzled sand castles at the beach. Sunlight danced and dazzled on the thin strip of the Salzach river, threading its way through the valley, peaceful and serene.

She was alone in the world right now and happy to be so.

An imp of mischief took hold and she spun around and around, dancing faster and faster until the wild flowers were a kaleidoscope of colours blurring against green and blue. Finally, laughing at her foolishness, she fell to the soft grass and lay back, gazing contentedly up at the deep blue sky.

Her hair spread around her, a riot of waves and tangles, rich chestnut against the green grass. She was in heaven. And had another full day before the duties of her job demanded her return. Demanded she shed this persona and resume the role she'd chosen so many years ago.

'Do you know you are trespassing?' a voice asked in German.

Melissa sat up abruptly and spun around to seek the source of the voice. She blinked when she saw the man, and wondered dazedly if she was dreaming. He moved slowly from the cover of the forest, riding a magnificent sorrel-coloured horse. The man sat on the horse as if he were part of him. Without visible signals, he urged his mount forward and stopped near Melissa, looking down at her without expression.

He looked like a Norse god, was her initial thought. His hair was a burnished tawny gold, highlights gleaming as if streaked from hours in the sun. His eyes were a clear cold blue, like alpine lakes. A small scar slashed across one cheek, not detracting from his looks, but making Melissa wonder what had happened. The chiselled features of his face blended well with the rugged mountains surrounding them. His broad shoulders and strong thighs matched the strength and splendour of the locale.

Melissa scrambled to her feet, brushing clinging bits of grass from her shirt, her shorts. She flicked a longing glance to her picnic blanket and her shoes. She wished she'd kept them on. Bravely facing up to the intruder, she looked up. A long way up. How tall he must be when off the horse; she could already tell he was a big man. And definitely not pleased to see her.

Still, Melissa was in a very good mood and would let nothing spoil it.

'Do you speak English?' Maybe he'd be more forgiving towards a tourist. If not, she could speak German fluently—after all it was Austria's national language.

'Yes. Doesn't change anything—you're still trespassing.' The switch in languages had not softened his clipped tone, though his accent was unmistakably English.

'You're English! Is this meadow yours? I didn't realise it belonged to someone. I should have, though. How could something as lovely as this meadow escape ownership through the years? It's beautiful.'

Her friendly smile had no effect on the man. He sat staring at her, his eyes steady, narrowed slightly in the sun's glare. His tawny hair was cut short, causing no distraction from his firm jaw, his tight lips. For a fleeting second, Melissa wondered if his face would soften if he smiled. Or crack.

'I don't want tourists picnicking on my land,' he said. 'There are parks in Salzburg you can use.'

'I don't blame you. If visitors didn't take care of it, in no time it could be ruined. But a small picnic by a fellow countryman couldn't hurt. Could it?' She cocked her head and stared back. She'd seen no signs forbidding her to use the meadow. Not that she was up to the laws of this country, but surely one picnic couldn't hurt.

'If I let one, others would follow.'

Just then a capricious puff of wind blew across the face of the meadow, skipping across the grass, causing the flowers to dance in response. It also caught the napkin from Melissa's blanket, sending it tumbling across the pristine setting.

'Oops.' She turned to run after it, glad for a moment's respite from the disturbing stare of the meadow's owner. She gathered the paper and balled it up, stuffing it in her back pocket. Turning, she trudged slowly back to him.

'See what I mean?' he said.

'Oh, pooh, I cleaned it up. I wouldn't leave any rubbish here; it would spoil things. Would you care for some lemonade?' She smiled up at him again, wondering if he'd take some refreshment. If so, it might mellow his attitude a little, which might gain her permission to stay a bit longer.

'I'm not thirsty. I'll just wait here until you remove yourself and your things,' he said inflexibly. His horse swished his tail against a fly, stamped his foot.

Like a warrior of old, she thought, eyeing him appreciatively as he sat on the large horse. The animal was well mannered, she had to give him that. He stood steady beneath his rider, gazing over the hillside, his tail swishing occasionally in the heat.

'Come on down and have some lemonade. It's good. I got it at the *Pension* where I'm staying. Besides, I'm not ready to leave just yet. Do you live here? You must if this is your meadow,' she said gently, watching his face for his reaction to her bold statement. She was starting to have fun.

And was rewarded. He frowned and leaned forward

menacingly. 'You have no choice in the matter. You are trespassing and I want you gone. Now.'

Melissa tossed her mane of hair back to stall for time. She took a deep breath and let it out, moving her eyes across the meadow, and out across the view of the mountains and the valley that held Salzburg.

'It's so pretty here. I'm on holiday for a couple of days and was just enjoying the solitude and beauty. I'm not hurting your land, Herr. . .?' She turned to look at him, her eyebrows raised in question. 'I guess it's Mr, right?'

'Terrell, Bret Terrell.' He moved his horse closer to Melissa and leaned over, holding her with his gaze. 'I think you'd better leave.'

She blinked in startled confusion. He was the man she'd come to Austria to see! They would be meeting over the negotiation table on Monday morning. Good grief, of all the people to meet on her holiday! Should she mention who she was? Would he be more inclined to let her stay? But she didn't want to be caught up in business—she was on holiday. For today and tomorrow, she was still just a tourist. Let her stay an anonymous one.

She eyed him critically. It was clear that he was used to getting his own way. And was probably spoiled because of it, Melissa thought as she saw signs of growing impatience on his part.

'After you have some lemonade, I'll leave,' she said softly, pulling her eyes away and moving quickly to kneel down on the blanket and open the Thermos. She was startled to find him beside her in only a moment. He held the reins of the horse in one hand and reached down to grasp her arm with the other, pulling her up to her feet. She carefully kept the cup from spilling as she swivelled around to face him.

'Watch it—you almost made me spill it. Here.' She thrust the cup to him, banging into his chest, her surprise at the strength therein reflected in her eyes.

'I don't want it. What I do want is for you to leave. Do I have to throw you off?' His voice was like steel. His hand gripped her firmly, but not harshly. Melissa felt the warmth of his fingers against her skin and deep within her a fluttering sensation built.

'In American cowboy movies, the cowboy can drop the reins and the horse won't move,' she said, flicking a glance at his horse then back to the owner, hoping he'd not notice her reaction to the touch of him, not notice how unnerved she felt suddenly.

'This is not America, and if I let the reins go he'd head for the stable,' Bret said with forced patience, as if placating a child.

Melissa's hand was still against his chest, her fingers tingling with contact with his body, his warmth penetrating the rough cotton of his shirt, heating her fingers, his heart steadily pounding against her. She wished she could drop the cup and splay her hand against his muscles, feel their contour, feel the heated texture of his skin beneath her hand. Swallowing, she looked up into his eyes, and promptly forgot what she was going to say as she was lost in the blue depths.

Melissa wasn't concerned with propriety and doing the right thing. She was on vacation and hurting nothing, had looked forward to this brief respite from the demands of her job, and she was not going to let anyone deny her the pleasure of the day.

Not even Mr Bret Terrell.

She didn't know how long they stayed like that, face to face, locked in each other's gaze, neither backing down. Suddenly the horse blew through his nostrils and nudged his master. The bump spilled the lemonade and broke the spell.

'Dammit!' Bret said, dropping Melissa's arm and futilely wiping at the sticky liquid now soaking his shirt.

'It'll dry in only a second. It's a wonderful day, warm and balmy. Even the grass is warm.'

That comment caused him to look at her bare feet, then leisurely examine her body as he brought his eyes back to her face—a perusal that must have met with his approval as his expression softened slightly.

Never one to let an opportunity slide, Melissa poured a little more lemonade into the cup and offered it again, careful to refrain from touching him. Though she wanted to, she wanted to see if she had imagined the sparks and heat from him.

'You never give up, do you?' he said. Surprising himself as well as Melissa, he took the cup and sipped the cold liquid. It was tart and tasty. He drank it all, his eyes never leaving hers. When finished he handed her the cup.

'Now will you leave?' One tawny eyebrow cocked as his voice caressed her. His tone was silky, coaxing, and Melissa's heart fluttered in response.

'Will you forcefully evict me if I don't?' she asked saucily. Her heart began to beat faster at the thought. Would he pull her up before him on his horse and race through the woods to the road like knights of old? Melissa's eyes began to sparkle at the idea.

'If I have to.' He sounded resigned.

She smiled delightedly again, a dimple flashing in her cheek, her eyes dancing in amusement and anticipation.

'Then yes, I'll pack everything up quickly. Then you can force me away, or carry me off on your horse. Won't that be fun?'

Melissa ignored the comment he made beneath his breath and packed her backpack with her picnic things. Donning her shoes, she slung the backpack on her shoulders and glanced around for one last view. It was still glorious.

'Ready,' she said brightly, challengingly, her chin tilted slightly as she stared up at him, daring him to do his worst.

'March. That way.' He pointed towards the path she'd followed when she'd first discovered the meadow.

'Oh, no, Bret Terrell, I want you to evict me forcibly. Otherwise I'm not going.' She sank to her knees on the grass and looked expectantly up at him, her eyes dancing in enjoyment, in mocking defiance.

'This isn't a game,' he ground out, his frown fierce.

'Sure it is. That's what makes life so much fun.'

'Life does not need to be fun. I could call the police.'

She knew the threat was hollow. Her smile was mischievous.

'Calling the police would be an adventure of a different sort. But unless you're carrying a portable radio with you I don't think I'd wait around for them to arrive.' She stood up in one lithe movement and reached out to touch his arm.

'Loosen up a little, Bret Terrell, I'm only teasing. But I would like a ride on your horse.'

Bret turned and mounted quickly. Without another word, he reached down his hand for hers and pulled her up behind him. Surprised at his sudden capitulation, Melissa put her arms around his waist and held on, letting her eyes stray across the meadow for one last time.

She was instantly aware of his warm body against hers, his back straight and muscular. His stomach was flat and strong beneath her hands, and she had a powerful urge to let her fingertips slip beneath his shirt and explore his taut skin. She took a deep breath, her breasts pressing against his back, and quickly exhaled in startled surprise. Where were her thoughts leading her? For heaven's sake, she was the daughter of a vicar—she had no business thinking such salacious thoughts about a man she just met, no matter how gorgeous and sexy she found him. No matter how his very warmth evoked dormant desire and longings within her. Dangerous feelings to one who had been burned once.

Bret urged the horse to a canter and Melissa held on for dear life, delighted with the turn of events, with the excitement of the afternoon. They crossed the meadow as if they were flying, then slowed as he guided the horse into the forest. The sunlight was dappled and the air immediately cooler. Melissa was glad she had his warm body to lean against, to keep the chill from her.

It was over too soon. In no time, they drew up beside her small rental car. He turned in the saddle, brushing one soft breast with his arm, sending waves of sensations through her nerve-endings.

'End of the line. Stay away from places that are off the beaten path in the future.'

Melissa slid down to the ground, clinging to his proffered hand a moment until her legs steadied.

'I won't you know. It's from the unexpected sometimes that life's greatest treasures are found. I enjoyed my lunch at your meadow, Mr Terrell. Maybe I'll see you there tomorrow.' She stared up at him but he didn't respond. With a sassy flip of her head, and a brief sketch of a wave, she turned and got into the car. From the rear-view mirror, she could see him still sitting on the horse as she drove away, staring after her. Was that a smile that touched his lips? She was too far away to know for certain

So that was Bret Terrell, the man she'd come to Austria to meet. Interesting to discover him outside of the office. Was he going to be difficult? It would be a challenge if so. But that was still two days away. Today she was on holiday. Melissa smiled, her happy mood expanding as she looked forward to the morrow.

Late the next morning Melissa pulled her rental car to the side of the road, in almost the same spot she'd parked the previous day. She glanced around, almost disappointed. She'd thought he'd be there to bar the way. But all she saw was the empty path that led to the meadow. It didn't matter. She really didn't think he'd come. She had just hoped he would.

Grabbing her backpack, she found the trail, walking quietly, enjoying the songs of the birds in the trees, the scamper of squirrels in the underbrush as she walked along the forest path. The scent of the fir and pine filled her nostrils, clean and fresh and pungent. Such a refreshing change from the dirt and grime of London. She took another deep breath. Could she bottle some of it to take home with her when her business in Austria was finished?

The meadow lay silent in the sun when Melissa left the confines of the forest, unchanged from yesterday. She gazed across the valley, her lips turning up involuntarily at the enchanting sight that lay before her. Others thought Vienna was the gem of Austria, but Melissa knew Salzburg was, with its baroque church spires, old parks, narrow streets and large open squares, and the beauty of the river beside it. She still had all of today to enjoy her holiday.

She chose a spot that captured the best view of the old city and took her blanket from her backpack, spreading it carefully over the grass, making sure she didn't damage any of the clumps of wild flowers that grew in such profusion. She wished she knew the names of them; some were vibrantly red, others a deep blue, pale yellow, or white. She'd like to pick them to take home and enjoy, but knew they would wilt and die before she reached her *Pension*. Instead, she would have to enjoy them here, in their natural setting.

'You're trespassing.' It was said in English.

She smiled before she turned to see him, gladness spreading through her. He'd come after all.

Bret Terrell was leaning against a tree, on foot today, watching her. He pushed off and started for her, his gait smooth and fluid, his long legs eating up the distance quickly, and his piercing blue eyes left hers only to roam over her face, glance at her long, shapely legs showing beneath her shorts, then returned to her face, her eyes.

'Hello, Mr Terrell. Come to throw me off again?' she asked, deliberately being provocative, her sassy grin belying her words.

He reached her blanket and easily sat down on the space she'd left.

'Doesn't seem to do me any good. You keep returning.' His lips twitched but he kept his face sombre.

'But only for today. It's the last day of my holiday. Then it's back to the salt mines.'

Melissa knew she looked good because she'd taken pains to do so, but she basked in the glances he shot her way. She had brushed her unruly hair until the curls were tamed and waves flowed flatteringly around her shoulders. She had carefully put on make-up that enhanced her own blue eyes but she suspected that the excitement of his presence caused the warmth in her cheeks.

'No horse today?' she asked as she delved into her backpack and began pulling forth food.

'No. Thought I might need both my hands.'

For a blinding moment Melissa considered what he could do with both hands—hold her face for his kiss, caress her, thread his fingers into her hair, touch her all over.

She closed her eyes and prayed for control. She tried to think of her father but Bret's face danced behind her eyes. Snapping them open, she thrust a sandwich towards him. Maybe coming here had been a mistake; maybe she was in over her head.

'I brought you roast beef.'

An eyebrow lifted. 'You were so sure I'd come?'

'No, only hoping. It's Sunday, so I thought maybe you wouldn't have to work and would like to share a bit of Austria with another visitor. I have a ham sandwich if you'd rather switch.'

His lips twitched and he shook his head. 'This is fine.'

Afraid to upset the tenuous balance, Melissa remained quiet though dozens of questions trembled on her lips.

'You didn't tell me your name yesterday,' he said.

'Melissa. Would you care for lemonade? I brought separate cups today.'

'Sure. Where are you from, Melissa?'

'London. Here.' She wished he'd touch her fingers when he took the cup, but he didn't. She sighed slightly and took a deep drink from her own cup. Maybe she should have brought just one cup, then they could have shared. The thought caused her to feel again the fluttering within her she had felt yesterday. Disturbed, she looked at the view.

'Visiting here on holiday?'

'Yes. Today's my last day. Then I have to go back to work. But I've had such a good time. I've taken the tour in the city, visited the Hohensalzburg castle, and found this wonderful place. I love the view from here,' she said, smiling at him shyly.

Bret finished the cookies she'd brought and lay back on his elbows, listening to her as she told him what she'd enjoyed and what she'd found unusual, watching the expressions dance across her face. His long legs stretched out and crossed at the ankle, he looked the picture of contentment.

'In fact——' Melissa carefully gathered up all the rubbish and put it away in her backpack, thankful that no wind today could toss it across the grass '—if I had all the money in the world, I'd buy this meadow from you and build a huge house here, all glass on one wall so I could see this view every day.'

He smiled at her. 'Only if I would sell.'

'Oh, but if I had all the money in the world you'd have to, to get some money to buy other things.' She giggled softly at her absurd picture, and was pleased when his smile widened.

'You're a nutty girl, Melissa,' he said, watching her as if puzzled by her.

'Others have said that, too. But I'm not, you know. I just try to enjoy myself. Life is so exciting, so full of promise. I love it.'

His look became arrested and he turned away. 'It shows.' His voice was no longer warm and friendly, but more formal, distant. What had she said to make him?

'Tell me something about you. You live here, obviously—why? What do you do? Do you have a house or camp out?' She would not let on that she knew a great deal about him, from his schooling to his assuming the leadership of Austerling Ltd., to the fact that he was a widower with a young child. She was curious to know what he'd tell her.

'My work is here. I run an electronics firm.'

'How did an Englishman come to run an Austrian firm?'

'It's a long story.'

'Tell me about your company,' she suggested, leaning back on her arms, studying him from beneath her lashes, almost flirting with him.

He smiled and shook his head. 'Another time perhaps.'

'Do you live near here?'

'I have a house near by, a very large, very old house. It does not have this view, but another that is equally impressive.'

'And as pretty?'

He glanced at her, his eyes drawn to her mouth. Melissa licked suddenly dry lips, yet smiled sassily at him, as if daring him to kiss her. As she waited for his next words, her eyes met his, her heart pounded in hopeful anticipation. For what?

'Almost as pretty,' he said slowly, bending his head towards hers, his gaze never leaving hers.

In the next moment Melissa was lying on her back, her hair spread out around her face, her view filled by Bret as he leaned over her, his hands gentle on her shoulders. He studied her face for a long moment, then slowly lowered his mouth to hers.

Melissa closed her eyes to better savour the feel of him. His lips were warm and hard against hers, moving persuasively until she responded. Her heart pounded and heated blood poured through her veins as if ignited from his touch. When he pushed through the barrier of her teeth, teasing her tongue, stroking it softly with his, he filled her with spiralling sensations of heady delight.

His hands threaded themselves in her soft hair and held her face for his pleasure. She relished the touch of his mouth against hers, his long fingers gently massaging her scalp, stroking the softness of her hair. She reached up to encircle his neck, feeling the weight of his chest come down on hers.

She was lost in the magic of the day, the enchantment of the setting, the joy of his touch. Her whole body came alive, vibrating, anticipating. Her heart beat heavily in her breast, her breathing became non-existent and the blood coursed through her veins in a hot riot of delight. She forgot where she was and why she'd come. She could only feel his mouth on hers, feel his hot lips against hers, feel the corded strength of his body beneath her searching fingers.

When Bret tilted her head to trail hot fire along her neck, she shivered. Then one large hand closed over her breast, massaging gently, tantalising the tip until it was hard and throbbing.

Warning bells began clamouring in Melissa's head. When his hand slipped beneath her top to find her swollen breast again, she pushed against him, struggling slightly to break the spell that caught them both.

'No,' she whispered when her mouth was freed. Good grief, what was she doing? She had to sit across from him at the negotiating table tomorrow morning! How would she be able to face him?

He pulled back slightly, his face hard. 'No?'

She shook her head slightly, regret evident in her expression, not that he saw it.

'Sorry, I really can't,' she murmured, her eyes touching his, then moving away in embarrassment.

He slowly pulled his hand from beneath her shirt and sat up.

'What game are you playing, Melissa?' His voice was hard and controlled, his face impassive.

Embarrassed, Melissa sat up, feeling the anger he directed towards her.

'I didn't plan that. I didn't know. . .'

'Don't give me that.' His voice was cutting. 'Women are born knowing. And especially English women. Is this some kind of revenge for being told to leave yesterday?'

'Of course not! I didn't kiss you, you kissed me!' she squeaked out, insulted that he'd think such a petty thing of her. Obviously the kiss had meant nothing to him.

'Go away *little girl*, and don't start things you're not willing to finish,' he said sardonically, his eyes contemptuous.

'I'm not a little girl and I didn't start that! I thought you would just kiss me. One kiss.'

'You're one green girl if you thought we'd stop at one kiss. Why else did you come back today? You knew I'd be here after that provocative display yesterday.'

'I thought you might be here. I hoped you would be. But only to share the day with. I wanted to have a good time and thought you needed to lighten up a bit. You're too serious.' She burned with embarrassment. Had he thought her so free and easy? Thought she'd come today just to make a play for him?

'You don't know me at all; just because I request a trespasser to get off my land doesn't make me "too serious".'

She couldn't tell him she knew much more than he

knew of her. All reports she'd ever seen depicted him as a serious, determined workaholic.

But none had mentioned how attractive he was. How she would enjoy meeting him, being with him. *How the touch of him would make her forget everything.* Lightly she rubbed her lips with her finger—they were slightly swollen. Licking them, she tasted Bret. She turned to look at him with startled eyes.

His gaze was on her, hooded, brooding, mocking. As if to call her 'little girl' again.

'I'm twenty-seven,' she said breathlessly, as if proving she were a mature woman because of age.

'I'm thirty-four; in contrast you seem a girl to me. Your reaction is that of a green girl. Are you sure you live in London?' His tone was mocking, his eyes icy blue.

'Yes, but that doesn't mean I'm free and easy with sex, especially with someone I just met!'

Scrambling to her knees, Melissa quickly packed her backpack, except for the blanket. He was still sitting on that.

'I'd better go.' Her lovely day had turned sour. Now she wanted to get away, wished she hadn't come. She wanted to recapture some of the feeling she'd had for this special place before today's events had turned everything upside-down.

'Run away, little girl. If you get experience, and want to play with the grown-ups, come back.' His mocking tone was hateful.

With one last look, Melissa turned and fled down the path towards her car.

CHAPTER TWO

MONDAY morning came too soon for Melissa when she awoke early. Her short holiday had passed swiftly and now it was back to work. She snuggled in the covers, remembering the four carefree days she'd spent in Salzburg. The image of Bret Terrell came unbidden, astride his magnificent horse, their ride through the forest, the picnic yesterday. For a long blissful moment she relived the kiss they'd shared on the mountain meadow.

Sighing in regret for the way the afternoon had ended, she rose at her accustomed hour and dressed for business. Today she'd see him in a totally different setting. Would he comment on their previous meetings? Or pretend they were newly met? Would she question why she hadn't mentioned her recognition of his name? She had not given him her last name. Would he have recognised it if she had? She was only one member of her company's team. Bret was the managing director of his firm.

It had been wonderful to take a small vacation. She wished she could have afforded more than four days, especially after meeting Bret Terrell. What would her vacation have been like had she met him on her first day? Would he have shown her parts of Salzburg, taken her dining or dancing? Probably not, if yesterday was anything to go by.

Dressing in her sombre dark blue suit, she tried to guess how he'd react when meeting her today. Had he wanted to see more of her? If he had known how to reach her, would he have called?

But they'd meet today, in different circumstances. Melissa, her boss, Derek Millan, and assorted members of their respective staff were scheduled to meet with Bret at ten.

Melissa brushed her hair back and braided it into a neat French braid. The severe style made her look older and more responsible. She lightly applied make-up, but not much, since Mr Millan was old-fashioned in his views and didn't approve of it. She had fallen in with his wishes long ago. The slightly tinted glasses she needed for fluorescent glare completed her attire. She was ready.

For a brief moment she stared at herself in the mirror. Was this the real Melissa Carmichael? A successful career woman who had worked her way up in a large corporation through dedication and hard work? Or was the real Melissa the carefree woman who had enjoyed herself so much the last few days?

She had done well thus far in a predominantly male field, and it was due to her serious determination to succeed. Grabbing her briefcase, she left the room without any more soul-searching.

Derek Millan was in his mid-fifties. He was second in charge of Larbard Industries, the huge conglomerate in the process of negotiating a deal with Bret Terrell's business for the exchange of stock between the two companies, and for purchasing the sophisticated electronic components that Terrell's firm was known for. The agreement in theory had been reached and now the two companies were meeting to work out the final details.

Mr Millan had insisted that Melissa attend. She was a financial analyst who had been leading the research team on the feasibility of the proposed deal with Austerling Ltd. Mr Millan had wanted her in on all facets of the negotiations. It also helped that she spoke German.

Melissa was the last to join the Larbard Industries contingency in the ornate lobby of the building that housed Bret's offices. She glanced around the old building as she walked towards the group that waited for her near the marble stairs leading to the upper floors. The outside had been a soft yellow stone with ornate carvings around the tall windows, the inside was quiet and dignified. It was quite a change from the glass and concrete high-rise that housed Larbard Industries in London.

'Wondered where you were,' Derek said in way of greeting. His grey hair gave him a distinguished appearance. He wore his years well and his manner commanded respect.

She nodded and hid a smile. Derek was not one for small talk. 'Still five minutes before we need to go up. I have all the information you requested. Have you met him yet?' she replied calmly.

'No. We've talked on the phone, but not face to face. Gerry, you have those charts on the financial growth?' he asked one of the junior executives flanking the group.

'Yes, sir, we're ready to show how it will——'

'Yes is all I wanted.' Mr Millan's short temper was excused by all below him. Although he was demanding and hardworking, he was fair and the people who worked for him always learned from him.

'Let's go up.'

He led the way to the lift, his personal secretary at his side. Melissa fell in behind them and hid a smile. She felt as if she was participating in a military operation. What would Bret Terrell think when they invaded his offices?

As the lift rose, she tried to imagine exactly what Bret Terrell would say when he saw her. She looked quite different from the woman he'd kissed yesterday. Would he be surprised to see her? Make some outrageous remark about their encounters in the meadow, or ignore having met her before? She was curious to see him in action, having read a description of the man that was circulated through the group before their departure from London. Derek believed it paid to understand your opponent to gain the best advantage.

The conference-room to which they were shown was luxurious. Deep charcoal carpet cushioned their feet, the papered walls were done in soft silver with maroon stripes. Mahogany table and chairs gave the room a staid, conservative air. Tall windows that covered one wall admitted bright sunshine into the room. The view was of the river, and the mountains surrounding the city, and the clear blue sky.

For a moment Melissa wished she were back at the meadow, enjoying the feel of the sun on her face and arms, the scent of the forest, rich and fresh, and the beauty of the vistas from the meadow.

But she was here to work. She took a seat three down from her boss and waited for Terrell's staff to join them. The seconds ticked by slowly. Yet in only moments the doors at the far end opened and Bret entered, leading a small coterie of assistants. Instantly the energy level in the conference-room sky-rocketed. Bret strode in like a conquering general, in charge, dynamic, almost arrogant. The other men in the room couldn't compete with his energy, or his looks. It was not only his size but his demeanour which gave him the edge.

Melissa was startled anew, staring at him. In a dark pin-striped suit, pale blue shirt and silver and navy tie he was formidable. His tawny hair was subdued in the office light, his tan deep, striking in contrast to the light shirt. He still looked like a Norse god, unexpected in corporate boardrooms. Yet this was a man in charge, in the boardroom as he had been in the meadow. Even Mr Millan seemed somewhat diminished.

Afraid of rousing interest from her own group, she dropped her gaze and rearranged her notepad and several folders containing the different estimates and quotes Mr Millan had asked for. She could not afford to be caught staring at Bret; it was unlike her, though hard to resist. When she looked up again, Bret was shaking hands with her boss.

'An honour, I'm sure. May I present my staff?'

'I have the list of everyone—Miss Stromford, Mr Toliver, Miss Carmichael, Mr Ross and you,' Bret said smoothly. 'As I'm sure, you have the list of my representatives.' He sounded impatient with the formalities and quickly nodded to the others, now seated.

'I think we both have plenty of people who can give us all the information we need, and work out matters to suit themselves. You and I need to discuss the overall strategy of the deal.' He set the ground rules, and expected all to follow.

Mr Millan looked at a loss for a moment. Melissa hid a smile. In England, he always took charge. Here, without even knowing how it happened, he'd been smartly outmanoeuvred by his host.

'I brought Miss Carmichael since she did most of the financial analyses for the proposed stock purchase, and she speaks German,' Mr Millan said, turning towards Melissa.

She looked up, now curious to see how he'd greet her. A tentative smile trembled on her lips.

Bret flashed her a quick glance, then paused, his gaze tightening slightly. For a long moment no one spoke. Melissa felt the heat rise in her face as she became aware of his icy gaze, aware of the curiosity of the others.

'Miss Carmichael, is it?' His voice was silky yet Melissa knew instantly that he was angry. She nodded and tried to smile, her heart thumping. Would he say something about yesterday?

His gaze dropped to her mouth, to her breasts. Was he remembering the feel of them? She flushed scarlet, feeling a pull of attraction at the memory of his hands against her skin, his mouth against hers.

'Speaks German, hmm?' His eyes pierced hers again. 'Excellent; she can lead this group then and assist where necessary. Not all of my staff are fluent in English, so her services won't be wasted.' He nodded politely, his eyes glittering at Melissa. She knew she'd not escaped completely.

Glancing around, Melissa saw only idle curiosity on the faces of her co-workers. She breathed a quick sigh of relief that Bret had not made any innuendoes regarding their previous encounters.

The negotiations proceeded on schedule. The various division managers and staff of Larbard Industries had prepared their forecasts and projections, and the marketing department had put everything up in beautiful charts and graphs and marketing materials to give the best impression to Austerling Ltd. It was now only a question of reviewing everything and getting Bret Terrell to sign the agreement.

The next two mornings the members of Larbard Industries' team met in the conference-room at ten.

Bret would arrive as well, offer a general greeting to all then take Derek Millan with him for separate meetings. Each morning his eyes raked Melissa, but he never spoke directly to her. He never spoke directly to anyone except Derek and two of his senior managers, Erich Meyer and Karl Müller.

Each morning Melissa grew a little more angry that he refused to speak to her, grew a little bolder when he'd stare at her, trying to provoke a response. He recognised her but continued to ignore her, and it infuriated her as the days passed. But she refused to rise to the bait. He knew who she was; he could speak if he wanted to. Once she licked her lips slightly as if to taste him again, their picnic vivid in her mind. She stared in his deep blue eyes and remembered how he'd looked when he kissed her. Awareness flared hot and evident in his eyes, but he refused to speak.

She was acting like a lovestruck teenager, she acknowledged. It was past time to get her mind on business and forget the man. The schedule called for two weeks, then she'd be gone. With hard work, could she shorten the time?

Thursday afternoon Melissa was summoned into the inner office. Mr Millan had some reports that Bret's staff had recently prepared and he wanted Melissa to read and summarise them to him. Her nerves on edge, she went to the office.

It was spacious, with a huge desk and chair near the windows. A sofa in muted tones occupied one wall, with a small conference table opposite. The walls were panelled in a rich dark wood, giving the office an ageless warmth not found in most modern buildings.

Derek Millan sat at the table, folders and papers spread out around him. Bret Terrell sat behind the desk, on the phone. His eyes hit Melissa as she entered.

Trying to ignore his narrowed gaze and the increase in her heart-rate, she quickly joined Mr Millan at the conference table.

'There you are,' he said as Melissa sat beside him. 'Read through these and give me the gist; don't analyse every number, just give me your overall assessment,' he told her impatiently.

A quick glance at Bret showed he was still watching her. Melissa turned back to the task in hand, took the report and scanned it, forcing herself to ignore the disturbing man. It was easy to tell her boss what it contained, and she summarised it so that he could understand the analysis readily. She kept her voice low so as not to disturb the room's other occupant.

Once or twice she swivelled slightly to see him from the corner of her eye. He now appeared totally engrossed in his work. Melissa didn't know whether to feel relieved or piqued.

When she had finished, she rose to return to the conference-room, throwing a quick glance at Bret.

'Finished?' he asked, rising with a thick folder in his hand. 'I have these papers for Karl; I'll walk with you.' His hard hand caught her arm and swung her towards the door.

Melissa stared up at him in startled surprise. They were soon alone in the hallway, the muted voices from the conference-room drifting out to them. The soft clatter of typewriter keys could be heard in the distance.

Bret's eyes glittered down at her and he snatched off her glasses, peering into her face, his tightening in anger.

'What the hell game are you playing, Miss Carmichael?' His anger was evident.

'I'm working.'

'How convenient that we met before.'

'That was an accident. Bret, you're hurting my arm.'

He eased his grip but didn't release her. His face was still angry. 'An accident? And Sunday, was that also an accident, or a not so clever way to find out more about my company to use to your advantage in the negotiations? How *convenient* to meet me accidentally before the meeting, and ask so casually about what I did for a living.' His voice was almost a sneer.

'I didn't do it deliberately!'

'Do you deny you knew who I was?'

'After you said your name I did,' she admitted, knowing he had a reason for his suspicions. It did seem suspect put the way he did. But it had been an innocent meeting. The first day.

Melissa licked her lips. 'But I didn't try to pump you for information. I was curious about you.'

His eyes focused on her mouth, as if he was recalling the kiss they'd shared. The brief enjoyment they had shared that day. And why she'd run away.

'What kind of disguise are you trying with this?' The hand with her glasses motioned to her hair.

She drew herself up to her full five feet six inches and raised her chin. '*This* happens to be the way I dress for work.'

'So the attire for the weekend is for play?'

Melissa knew he meant to be insulting.

'The way I dress when on holidays is my own affair.' Damn, wrong word to use. She knew that instantly when his eyes gleamed at her.

Melissa brushed his hand away, her fingers tangling with his for a moment. She was flustered and tingly from his attention, and touch. Darting her glance left and right, she saw that they were still alone in the corridor. Didn't he have a telephone call to answer, or a letter to dictate?

'You didn't tell me at the meadow that you spoke German. Or that we would be meeting again on Monday.' His voice was low almost seductive.

'I have to get to work.' Her voice sounded breathless. He was right and she didn't fully understand her reasons now for any of it. Nor did she understand the sensations racing through her at his closeness. Surely she was immune to charming men by now. She should remember the past.

He stared down at her for a long moment. 'Very well, return to work. But come and see me after. I'll be in my office.' It was not a request but an order.

Melissa hesitated.

'If you don't promise to come, I will haul you back now and demand from Derek Millan an explanation of his subordinate's actions.' His voice was hard, his eyes unflinching.

'You wouldn't dare!' But of course he would. He hadn't got to the top of his career by bluff only.

'Try me.'

'All right, I'll come around five-thirty.' Her eyes locked with his.

Bret handed her back her glasses and watched silently as she put them back in place. He didn't move as she turned and walked quickly to the conference-room. As Melissa passed through the doorway, she glanced back. He stared after her, his expression enigmatic, giving nothing away. She turned away, refusing to let him know he bothered her.

All afternoon Melissa worried about the coming meeting. She'd done nothing wrong, precisely. But it would have been courteous last weekend to tell him who she was, and the relationship she had with Larbard

Industries, especially once she'd learned his name. Too late now. She would just have to make him understand when she met with him. Though she wasn't quite sure she understood herself.

The time passed quickly and before she was ready the others began gathering up papers and making signs that they were leaving.

'Coming, Melissa?' Joe Ross asked as he snapped shut his briefcase.

'No, not just yet, I've a few more things to finish up.' She shuffled some papers before her and smiled brightly at her co-worker. One by one they left the conference-room, both the Austrians and the English, until she was alone.

Feeling much as if she was going to an execution—her own—she snapped shut her briefcase and pushed back her chair, heading for Bret's office.

Knocking softly, she opened the door when he snapped out a brief, 'Come.'

'We're finished for the day,' she said, standing in the doorway. Derek Millan had gone; Bret was alone.

'Come in.'

Melissa stepped in and closed the door behind her, moving nervously into his office. The buildings visible from his windows were bathed in the late afternoon sun, shimmering softly beneath its rays. Here and there the sun reflected off the glass like diamonds.

'How lovely.' She smiled and moved to the window to see more, leaning her case against the wall. Anything to postpone the coming confrontation.

Bret rose and joined her, standing by her side. 'It's a beautiful city, and not as crowded as London, eh?'

'Yes. Though London is beautiful as well,' she said quickly, conscious of his presence.

'Yes, it is. I miss it. But I'm stuck here for a few

more years. Why do you scape your hair back so unbecomingly?' He asked as his fingers went to the clip at the base of her braid and released it.

'Hey.' She turned to find herself almost in an embrace as his hand remained in her hair, his arm now encircling her. She held her breath a moment, so close she could touch him with scarcely any movement on her part.

His eyes flicked down to hers, then back at the task at hand. In a moment he'd released her hair from the confines of the French braid and ran his fingers through the chestnut tresses, massaging her scalp slightly, threading through the soft waves and curls, spreading it around her shoulders, enjoying the soft texture against his fingers. Then he slipped off her glasses.

'I'm not some doll to play with,' she said, annoyed that he thought he had the right. Stepping back, Melissa tried to put some distance between them.

'No, you're not a doll. Why do you scrape your hair back?'

'I want to present a professional look for business. How professional do I look now?' she asked.

He studied her for a long moment, then smiled slightly. 'Not very, but infinitely more approachable.'

'Approachable? You're a fine one to talk. You're like a general locked up in some holy shrine with everyone too afraid of you to get near enough even to ask a question.' Melissa had learned that the best defence would be to take the offence. She didn't trust being with him, didn't trust herself if he touched her. She wanted him to think about something else, not about her.

He frowned. 'Afraid of me? What are you talking about?'

'We needed some information today, and your managers didn't have it. But instead of asking you they went around polling others, interrupting several people trying to get the information. We wouldn't do something like that in Larbard.'

'They could have come and asked me.'

'No, they were too afraid of your reaction. I don't think you're very approachable,' she said.

'That's never been a problem. Maybe you're making too much of it.' He frowned slightly as he considered what she'd said.

Melissa didn't know if her hair down made her more approachable, but it made her more conscious of her own femininity. She turned to look out of the window, seeing a hint of her reflection on the glass. Her hair swirled around her face, across her shoulders. She looked as if she was still on holiday, not at all like the firm, conservative businesswoman she'd tried so hard to become.

'Come to dinner with me tonight,' Bret said. 'We can discuss this approachability fault you think I have.'

'But I. . .'

He put his fingertips on her lips. 'No, don't argue, just come with me.' He left his fingers against her lips until she nodded slightly, then brushed them back and forth once before dropping his hand.

'Are you ready now?'

'I can be. There is more to do, but tomorrow will suffice.' She put her hands up to confine her hair.

'Leave it as it is. I like it that way.'

'But it's so wild.'

'No, it's not.' He threaded his fingers through her hair and combed it slightly, smiling as he looked down at her. 'It looks charming. Leave it. Since it's early, we'll walk. I know a quaint little place you'll like.'

He was right, Melissa thought as they entered the

old-world retaurant. The lower floor of the building was stone and wood and obviously hundreds of years old, yet cosy and relaxing. The tables were wide-spaced, affording privacy to the diners. They were seated at a secluded table near the back, in a small alcove. Melissa smiled her pleasure with the setting as Bret looked across at her.

'It's perfect.'

'And the food's good, too.' He smiled his own satisfaction.

Once they'd ordered, Bret leaned back, his face serious, his eyes intent. 'Now, Miss Melissa Carmichael, why don't you tell me about your reasons for keeping your identity secret last weekend?'

She studied her hands as if looking for the answer, then raised her face to his, matching his serious tone.

'It's hard to explain right now. I guess I felt you'd behave differently towards me if you knew who I was. It was an accident, our meeting like that, a strange coincidence. Yet I didn't know if you'd view it as such.'

'A little too opportune, don't you think?' he murmured smoothly.

'See, that's what I thought you'd think. I just stopped the car, followed the path and found the meadow. I didn't expect anyone there. I was just exploring.'

'On Saturday maybe. But on Sunday you came back knowing who I was and obviously expected me back as well.'

'Hoped, more like.' She grinned at him. 'I was glad you came back without your horse. Parts of the picnic were fun, don't you think?' For a moment she was that carefree tourist. She could almost feel the soft air and warm sun as she had last Sunday.

He glanced at her lips and Melissa felt as if he'd kissed her again. She looked away.

'Parts were fun. Deliberately set up, however.'

'No! Just a chance to meet you in an informal setting. And I'm glad I did. You're formidable at the office. And not very approachable.'

'Ah, the approachability issue. Who was it who needed the answer and was afraid to come to me?'

'Karl Müller.'

'Curious. He has been with the firm for many years. He knows I always have time for him. What was the issue?'

'Something to do with a German company that owns some shares of stock. You apparently did a similar deal with that firm a few years ago.'

'True. I'm entitled to do so.' His voice hardened.

'I never said you weren't. Did Karl also object to that deal?'

'Object? What do you mean?' Bret frowned at her question.

'I mean he's very much opposed to the deal we are working on and does what he can to delay it.'

'Nonsense. He's a loyal employee. He was here when I took over. Karl knows the deal is good for both our firms. It'll open new opportunities for us in England and we need the expansion.'

Melissa shrugged and looked up as the waiter approached with the soup. 'Nevertheless, he's against, as is Erich. Neither is as co-operative as he should be.'

Bret's expression hardened. 'I hardly think you are the expert on how my managers do their jobs. Our firm is committed to this deal and we are working towards that end. Perhaps you are too new at negotiations to understand the nuances.'

'I've been working in similar situations for over four years, Mr Terrell; I do know what I'm doing, and can recognise delaying tactics.' Her voice was cool.

When Bret refused to credit her observation, she fell silent, frustrated and annoyed. Did he think she was deliberately stirring up trouble? Didn't he care about how the negotiations were going?

With the arrival of food, the topic of conversation changed. The charged atmosphere eased. Melissa asked questions about Salzburg which Bret readily answered. She was curious about Mozart and the early history of the city. She wanted to know about the problems the residents faced during the long winter months with the deep snow, and how long he'd lived in Salzburg.

'Do you like living here?' she asked, knowing it was a personal question, but curious to learn more about the man.

Immediately he changed, withdrew. Obviously, personal questions were not allowed.

'It's tolerable. I came when offered the managing director's position. I've been able to expand the company quite a lot in the last ten years. Maybe with the greater expansion into England because of our deal I'll be able to move the headquarters there one day.'

'Is your family in England?' Melissa wished she knew more about him. The dossier the marketing department had produced focused on his business life, barely touched on his personal life.

'My mother and sisters live in England with their families.'

'Was your wife from here?'

His face closed and he looked away, pain and anger clearly visible.

'My wife was also from England.' His answer was abrupt, short. 'Do you care for dessert or shall we leave now?'

Melissa was taken aback. Obviously the loss of his

wife was still painful. She thought his wife had died several years ago.

'I'm sorry,' she said softly.

He looked at her then, a sardonic smile twisting his lips. 'For what? Prying into my personal life? So like a woman. It wasn't secret at the time. She tried to kill us both and only succeeded in killing herself.' He lightly touched the scar that ran across his cheek. 'This is my legacy. But I still have my life.'

Melissa was horrified. Good grief, what had happened? Had his wife really tried to kill them both? How? Questions trembled on her lips, but one look at his glittering eyes and she kept quiet.

'I do not care for dessert, thank you. I should be returning to my hotel. I have enjoyed the evening.' Melissa sounded like the polite little girl her mother had raised.

Bret summoned a waiter for the bill and in a short time they arrived at the small *Pension* where Melissa was staying. She did not stay at the same hotel with the others in her group, preferring to keep her own time to herself and not be talking shop all the time. The rooms of the *Pension* were large, with lofty ceilings and dark hardwood floors, furnished with homey comfortable furniture. Melissa found them charming, and more restful than conventional hotels.

Bret had the cab wait while he escorted her to her door.

'Perhaps you would care to have dinner with me again tomorrow?' he said as he took the key from her fingers and opened her door for her.

Melissa almost leapt at the opportunity, but something held her back. She could feel the pull of attraction she'd felt at the meadow. A dangerous attraction. She'd do better to keep her distance. She was here for only a few more days and then would be returning to England. She didn't want to get caught up with Bret Terrell.

'I already have plans,' she temporised, knowing that eating alone would never be as enjoyable as another evening with Bret. But it was safer, wiser.

'Would you care to go riding with me Saturday?'

'I'd love it.' She spoke before she could think. It would be wonderful to go riding with Bret. Her face lit up with pleasure and she nodded. If the weather was nice, maybe they could go to the meadow for a picnic. Was his house far from the meadow?

'I'll pick you up at nine. Wear something comfortable. Do you have boots?'

'Not with me.'

'I think a pair of my sister's will fit you.'

Without another word, he leaned over and kissed Melissa lightly on the lips.

'I'll see the formidable Miss Carmichael in the morning, I'm sure, but will eagerly await Saturday to see the young carefree Melissa who dances in the meadow,' he said softly.

Turning, he was gone in an instant. Melissa smiled dreamily as she glided into her room and shut her door behind her.

CHAPTER THREE

WHEN Melissa stepped from the lift the next morning, one of the secretaries for Austerling Ltd met her with a shy smile.

'Mr Terrell would like to see you in his office before you go to the conference-room,' she said formally. 'He'll be there in just a minute.'

Melissa glanced across the open work area, seeing Bret near the desk of an older woman. He was laughing at a comment she had made. For a moment he seemed years younger and carefree. Melissa smiled, wishing he'd laugh with her like that. Maybe on Saturday.

With a nod of thanks to the secretary, Melissa headed down the hall to Bret's office. Her briefcase was still in there. He probably wanted to return it to her before work started. But she couldn't help the increase in her heartbeat at the thought of seeing him alone for a few moments.

Bypassing the conference-room, Melissa walked quickly to Bret's office. The door stood open and she entered. Seeing her briefcase against the wall beneath the window, she crossed the room to retrieve it.

'I'd forgotten that. You'll need it, of course.' Bret entered behind her, towering over her, his presence seeming to fill the room. 'Your hair's tied up again.'

'Of course, I'm working.' She tried to ignore how her heart sped up when he drew near. She took a breath.

'I don't like it that way.'

'Sorry.' Her tone belied the word.

'Melissa, take it down, you look much prettier,' he said, leaning against the desk, his eyes amused as he watched her.

'I can't. And you still have my glasses. I need them because of the glare.' She bravely walked over to stand before him. Staring up at him, she couldn't help remembering last night, the feel of his lips against hers, the fleeting kiss they'd shared. She glanced involuntarily at his lips and then looked up into his eyes, blushing at his knowing look.

'I'll return the glasses if you let down your hair.' His voice was low, caressing.

'Bret, just give me the glasses.' She held out her hand.

He reached into his coat pocket and pulled them out, but instead of handing them to her he opened them and gently placed them on her nose. His hands continued to the back of her head and in only a moment had undone the clip and released her hair.

'Bret!' Her hands tried to keep the braid, but his fingers were busy combing through the soft curls, and in no time the tresses were waving around her face in a cloud of chestnut, golden highlights gleaming in the morning light.

'I like it better that way,' he said softly, and leaned over, lightly brushing her lips with his. 'Leave it like that, Melissa, please.' His voice was low, beguiling, entreating. 'We will all still be impressed with your ability at work, but you'll look more *approachable*.'

She laughed as he turned her words back and shook her head. It did feel better to let her hair go free. What would her co-workers think, however? Oh, well, it was a small thing he asked. The way she felt right now, she'd give him anything he requested.

'All right, but if I get any sly innuendoes I'll brush it right back.'

'If you get any, tell me and I'll settle it!' he said arrogantly. Standing, he nodded towards the door.

Melissa led the way towards the conference-room. 'We should be finished by next week,' she said, searching for conversation to fill the awkward silence.

'And then you'll return to London?'

'Yes. I've already had a holiday.'

'Pity,' was all he said before opening the door and ushering her inside.

Melissa's colour was high as she faced a dozen pair of eyes as she and Bret entered the conference-room together. There was rampant speculation, she could see, as the others glanced at the two of them, but no one said a word.

The rest of the day proceeded as the earlier ones had and Melissa was only slightly disappointed when she left at the end of work without having seen Bret again. It was her own fault; she'd had the opportunity to dine with him and refused. Now she would have to live with that. Only she hadn't realised how much she wished he had asked her again. She might not have said no a second time.

Bright and early on Saturday Melissa was up and dressed, ready to go riding. She wore a pair of old soft jeans that moulded her figure like a second skin. Her shirt covered a sleeveless Lycra top and she left the buttons of the shirt undone, knotting the ends in front. Her hair sparkled and shone in the light.

Promptly at nine Bret pulled up before the *Pension*. Melissa hurried out to greet him and slipped into the black BMW before he could get out.

'Good morning,' she said brightly, smiling her happiness.

'In a hurry?' he asked mockingly, turning slightly in the seat to see her better, his eyes roaming over her figure. His eyes widened slightly when he saw the gap between her shirt and jeans, the alabaster of her skin, and his hands tightened on the wheel.

'Didn't want to hold you up,' she said. 'Or keep the horses waiting.'

He grinned as he set the car in motion and pulled away from the kerb, pointing out some of the sights of interest as they passed through the old town. Soon they were climbing towards his home.

The scenery was beautiful and Melissa enjoyed the drive, her attention split between the loveliness of the view and the man beside her. He handled the car competently, his hands strong and assured on the wheel. His shirt and jeans were both a pale blue which deepened the blue of his eyes. She studied his profile, then looked beyond him, out of the window, so that he would not know she was studying him.

She wished she could trace his eyebrows with her fingertips, brush them against his lips, feel the texture of his cheeks, the firm line of his jaw. . .feel the strength of his muscles, the warmth of his skin against hers.

Abruptly she shifted in her seat and looked the other way. Thoughts like that would get her into trouble. She was only going for a ride.

The sweet bay mare Bret had picked out for her was perfect. Melissa donned his sister's boots and hurried to mount. The mare was named Schönfeld—pretty meadow—and Melissa threw him a suspicious look. Was Bret a romantic?

He came around to see how the stirrups fitted and looked up at her, seeing her amusement.

'Now what?' he asked. His head tilted back, his

shoulders broad and his feet planted firmly on the floor of the barn, he looked like a conqueror. Melissa caught her breath, her heart-rate speeding up.

'I was wondering if you're a romantic. This horse's name reminds me of the pretty meadow where we met.'

'Alas, it has been her name since she was born. But if you care to think it. . .'

'Let me keep my fantasies; I'm a romantic and I'm not ashamed of it. Are we riding today, or what?'

'We ride.' Bret mounted the big sorrel gelding he'd ridden when Melissa first met him and led the way from the stable towards the woods.

The ride was exhilarating. They rode through the forest, then out across the meadow where they'd first met. Crossing it, Bret led her higher and higher, pausing now and again for Melissa to gaze at the vistas that lay before them. The air was clear and clean, the day warm and sunny, and the two of them were alone on the mountainside with only the horses.

They talked easily about the countryside, how it compared to other countries they had visited and other hillsides. Melissa stayed away from asking any questions of a personal nature, not wanting to put a damper on the day, remembering his response at dinner. But she was not loath to let Bret know some of her background. She was outrageous in her recounting of trail rides she had gone on in Wyoming when she had visited her mother—doing her best to entertain him.

'She was so lonely after Dad died. Then she decided to visit a dude ranch in Colorado. Jason was there on business and they fell in love and got married, all in three weeks.'

'Were you upset?' Bret asked curiously.

'Not after I met Jason. He's a peach. And to see the

two of them together is wonderful. I hope I can have a marriage like that. Mum and Dad were happy, I always thought. But she's radiant now with her new love.'

'You two are close?'

'Yes. Though she didn't wait for me to get there for the wedding.' Melissa laughed. 'No matter. I'd have been a fifth wheel. But when I did go to visit, I learned a lot about ranching—and went on those flaky trail rides.'

Melissa shared her life with Bret, telling him amusing stories about work, about her flat in London, about growing up as a vicar's daughter. The morning flew by and before she realised it they were back at the stable.

'That was wonderful,' she said once she'd dismounted. Throwing her arms around Bret, she gave him an enthusiastic hug. She'd had a marvellous time.

His arms came around to catch her close, holding her body stretched out against his, her arms still around his neck. His hand sought the strip of skin beneath her shirt, his fingers gently rubbing her softness.

'You're playing with fire, little green girl,' he murmured as he held her against him.

Melissa looked up at him, a smile settling on her face. 'Am I?' she asked provocatively, her heart pounding again at his nearness. Her body felt the heat of his along her length and she could not have moved for anything. She was not quite as green as he thought, but there was no need to tell him that.

He nodded emphatically and dropped his arms, his hand grabbing one of hers.

'The stable is not the place.' Nodding to the stable boys who were grooming the horses, he led her towards the house.

Melissa made no protest, walking quickly to keep up with him, anticipation bubbling up inside her. She was having such fun! Who would have thought her day with Bret would go along these lines?

After the bright sun light the house seemed dim and dark. Her eyes had scarcely begun to adjust to the dimmer light when he pulled her into a study and firmly closed the door.

He swept her into his arms and bent his head to kiss her. His lips were warm and hard against hers as he moved against her softness, coaxing a quick response from her. With a soft sigh, she settled against him, moving her lips to enjoy his touch.

His tongue teased her and Melissa parted her lips to admit him. She flared up as if in flames when his tongue met with hers. She was only vaguely aware of the heat from his body as he moulded her to him, her own was so hot! She was caught up in the fire and delight of his mouth against hers, the thrusting seeking of his tongue, the tantalising pressure of his lips moving against hers. She clung to him as the kiss deepened.

Finally Bret pulled back slightly, breathing hard, his eyes glittering, demanding as they roamed across her face, settling on her wet, swollen lips with deep satisfaction.

'I think you've bewitched me,' he said softly, his eyes taking in the high colour in her cheeks, the sparkle in her eyes.

'I think you have enchanted me. Do they have enchanters in Austria?' she said, leaning forward to kiss him again.

He leaned against the door and pulled her closer. Melissa threaded her fingers through his thick head of hair, revelling in the feeling. She moved sensuously against him, and heard his soft moan in her ears. When one of his hands slipped beneath her loose shirt to trace her spine, she sighed with pure pleasure. She could feel the heat beneath her, the hardness of his muscles against her softness. She could feel his arousal and for a moment gloried in the feminine delight of her power over him. It had been years since she'd given so much to a man, years since she'd wanted to. Bret was flooding her with sensations and sensuous delights she'd never experienced before.

When his hand moved around to cup her breast, her breathing became laboured. A voice of caution sounded in her head. She must stop. Remember last time, she told herself.

Slowly, not wanting to end the pleasure, but determined not to repeat mistakes of the past, Melissa drew back. His hand on her breast was hot yet gentle and compelling. The spiral of delight deep within her was caused only by his touch. She hated to end it. But she must.

Bret moved to kiss her neck, his hand pressing her hips tightly against him, knowing she felt his hardness, wanting her to know how she affected him. Wanting her.

'Bret,' Melissa whispered, her hands now on his shoulders, pushing slightly against him.

'Mm?' His lips caressed her throat, his tongue flicked out to touch the pulse point, its heat almost her undoing.

'Bret, we have to stop. You're going too fast for me.' She pushed harder.

He raised his head, his hands stilled. 'I want you, Melissa. And I can tell you want me.' He gazed down at her, his face hard and still, his hand like a brand on her hip.

'Maybe, but that doesn't mean we're going to make love.' She pushed against him again, but he held her firmly.

'What kind of game are you playing?' His voice was harsh, his eyes narrowed as he stared down at her.

'No game. I wanted to kiss you. I like kissing you, touching you, having you touch me. But you're going too fast. Kissing's all I want to do.'

'I could have you down on that couch in no time, and you wouldn't refuse.' His eyes held hers as he spoke, his hand caressed her breast, fondling the nipple, sending waves of desire and heat and longing coursing through her.

'I would tell you no,' she said bravely, leaning against him, afraid of the feelings he was causing her. Afraid that maybe he was right and she couldn't tell him no. It wasn't fair; she hadn't asked for this strong pull of attraction, especially to someone she'd just met.

Bret dropped his hands and sagged against the door. Melissa leaned against him, dropping her head against his chest, closing her eyes, hearing the rapid beat of his heart. She didn't want to stop, but knew she must.

'Why?' he asked. He reached for her arms, pushing her back so that he could see her.

She dropped her eyes and said nothing. Embarrassment brought colour to her cheeks. She didn't want him to think she'd been leading him on just to tease.

'I just can't,' she murmured, staring at the brown column of his throat. 'We don't know each other very well. Our lives are too different. . .' She trailed off. How could she say she was too afraid of being hurt again? She projected a strong image; she couldn't let it slip now.

'I'm not asking for a lifelong commitment,' he said, his anger evident in his tight jaw, his narrowed glacial eyes.

'I'm not asking for it either. But neither am I someone to sleep around. I want love first.'

'And you accuse me of being romantic. What if you never fall in love?' he asked, still leaning against the wall, watching her from narrowed eyes.

'Then I won't,' she snapped out, not at all liking the way the conversation was going. She'd said no; did they have to keep discussing why?

'No man would expect a woman of your years to be a virgin on his wedding night,' Bret said slowly, thoughtfully.

'Oh, that's a fine line. And there's no worry about that. Sex is overrated. I'm not sleeping with you!'

'It wasn't a line.' He straightened and towered over her, his anger surging. 'What do you know about sex anyway, little girl?'

'That's none of your damn business! But I've been down that road before. Men just use women for their own ends. You want me, you just said so. Now you've come up against a roadblock and you want to get around it. I don't care what someone would or would not expect—I'm not sleeping with you!'

'I could make you.'

'Force me?'

'No, I would never force a woman.' He took a step closer and leaned over to capture her lips with his. He didn't touch her except on her mouth and Melissa knew he was testing her.

Involuntarily she responded, caught up again in the delight of his touch, the remembered feelings he brought her surfacing, and she swayed towards him. When she felt his lips smile in triumph, she came back to earth with a jolt.

Pulling back, she stared at him in dismay. 'No!' She stepped around him to get to the door. Was this the end of their day?

'You're a tease,' he ground out at her.

Melissa slammed the door behind her, affronted that he'd called her a tease. She was not. She was honest, she liked their kissing, but he was going too fast and far for her. Couldn't they have progressed at a slower pace? Maybe developed a friendship, more than friendship. Damn, why was she attracted to him. Life would be so much easier if she'd never met him.

Of course Bret had never hinted at anything like friendship. Maybe his experience with his wife was too awful for him to consider developing any kind of relationship. He wanted to have sex with her, nothing more.

And she—she couldn't trust herself. She'd made a mistake in judgement once before. Thought she'd been in love, but it had proved false. She dared not chance it again. The thought was depressing.

Melissa stood by the study door wondering how she was going to get back to her *Pension*. Could she call a cab, or would Bret take her back when he'd cooled down? She caught a flicker of motion from the corner of her eye. Looking up the stairs, she saw a small boy, sitting on the top stair, leaning against the railing.

'Hello,' she said, smiling

He looked so solemn.

Melissa climbed the stairs and sat beside him, knowing this was Bret's son. He looked like his father, same tawny hair, same blue eyes. He was adorable.

'I'm Melissa,' she said as she sank down.

'How do you do? I'm Maximilian Terrell.' He held out his small hand and Melissa hid a smile as she formally shook his hand.

'Your name is bigger than you are. Can I call you Max?'

He considered it for a moment and then nodded,

smiling shyly. 'Sure, that's what my father always calls me. I'm hoping to see him today,' he confided, looking up at Melissa seriously.

'Hoping to see him?' Melissa was confused.

'Yes. We usually spend the weekend together, only he had something important to do today. But maybe it won't take all day. Do you think it will?' he asked, turning back to look expectantly down the stairs at the door to the study.

She was the important thing to do today. Melissa began to feel guilty for taking Bret's time. He should have spent the day with his son, not romancing her. She studied the little boy and remembered her own father. He'd always been so glad to see her whenever she sought him out. Was Bret that way too?

'He's alone in the study now, why don't you go see him?' she suggested.

'Greta says not to disturb him.'

'Who's Greta?'

'My nursery maid.'

The door of the study opened suddenly and Bret strode out, searching the hallway for Melissa. When he caught sight of her sitting beside his son, he stopped, his fists on his hips, his body suddenly still, waiting as he looked back and forth between Melissa and Max.

'See,' Melissa said softly, 'here's your dad now. I bet he's glad to see you. Let's go down.' She stood and held out her hand. In only a moment, Max took it and stood up. Slowly they descended the stairs, Melissa conscious of Bret's regard the entire way.

'I see you've met Max.'

'Yes, he was waiting to see you. I've told him you're free now and would be glad to see him.'

Bret's face hardened, his eyes showed his anger. 'So now you lecture me on how to deal with my son?'

'No, I'm sure you are as successful there as with business. But he's been waiting to see you. There's no reason not to spend time with him, is there?'

'No, except I had planned to spend the day with you.' His gaze dropped again to her mouth, still swollen from his kisses. Melissa smiled tentatively, some of the tension leaving her.

'I'll stay, then, and you can spend the day with both of us. You can take me back after supper.'

'Dad?' Max said as he watched the exchange between the two adults.

Bret looked down at his son and smiled 'OK, son, we'll both spend the day with Melissa. Will you like that?'

'Sure, that'll be great; I can show her my soldiers.' The huge smile filled the boy's face.

'I'd like that.' Melissa smiled and leaned over to give the boy a quick kiss on his cheek. 'I used to play soldiers when I was a little girl.'

'Men want hugs and kisses too,' Bret said, looking at her.

'Then I will give you some more later. But only kisses.' Her eyes held his for a long moment. Then she looked away. 'Right now we need to spend time with Max.'

'Are you trying to take over my household, Miss Carmichael?'

Melissa shook her head. 'No, Mr Terrell. Now give your son a kiss and I'll give you one.' She grinned at his slow look, feeling much braver in the young child's presence. Safer.

Bret reached down and picked Max up, tossing him in the air, then holding him easily as he gave him a kiss on his young cheek. Turning, he stared down at Melissa. Holding out his other arm, she moved in and he pulled her close to kiss her on the cheek too.

'That's until later,' he promised.

She shivered slightly in anticipation.

CHAPTER FOUR

'HAVE you had your lunch yet?' Bret asked Max.

'Yes, sir. Greta gave it to me at noon.' The little boy was happy to be with his father and Melissa was fascinated by the change in Bret. He obviously enjoyed spending time with his son. And the boy adored his father.

'Well, Miss Carmichael and I haven't yet eaten. I was just going to let Marta know it's time for our lunch.'

'She said I could call her Melissa,' Max said, looking at Melissa.

'I certainly did. Why don't you run up to the nursery while we eat, then your dad and I will come up afterwards to play games with you, or read to you or whatever you wish?' Melissa suggested.

'Will you, Dad?' he asked, his eyes sparkling in delight at the suggestion.

'If Melissa said so, it is so.' Bret's eyes glittered at Melissa, and she swallowed hard. She didn't think he was pleased. Was it so different from his plans for the day? Had he thought to have them spend it in his bed? She thought she'd been clear about that before.

Bret watched as his son scampered up the stairs then turned to Melissa.

'That was not how I planned our day,' he said drily.

'Little boys need attention. He's used to spending time with you on the weekends. I don't want to be the cause for that to change,' she told him, holding his look with her own, tilting her chin determinedly, not backing down an inch.

'Big boys need attention too,' he said again, looking at her mouth.

Melissa let her amusement show as she put her arms up around his neck and leaned against him slightly. 'Maybe we could have the hugs and kisses you want later. But we should spend this afternoon with your son.'

He reached around her and pulled her tightly against him, lowering his mouth to hers for a hard, brief kiss.

'I'll hold you to that!'

She looked up at him, her face serious. 'But only hugs and kisses, Bret.'

'You made that clear earlier.' He hugged her briefly then set her back. 'Tell me what happened to you with that other man.'

Melissa paled, pulling away from him. 'What do you mean?'

'In the study you mentioned knowing all about sex, and how men only use women. It must be from experience, right?'

'It's none of your business,' she stalled.

'I'm making it my business. Tell me.'

She stared at the floor, heat flooding her face. Her quick mouth got her into more trouble than anything. She didn't want to tell Bret, didn't even want to think about Brian ever again.

'Melissa?' His finger lifted her chin until her sky-blue eyes were gazing into his deep blue ones. He stared down at her, compelling in his desire to learn what she would tell him.

'I thought I was in love, but he only wanted to make another woman jealous.' The pain couldn't be hidden.

The hurt and confusion washed through her again as she remembered the awful betrayal of all she held dear.

'I don't offer love, but I would never lie to you. And the pleasure you'd feel would be real and true,' he said softly, his thumb brushing lightly back and forth against her lips.

Slowly she shook her head. She couldn't do it, much as her body longed for his touch, longed to feel the ecstasy she knew Bret would give her.

He straightened, and turned away. 'Let's go eat.'

Melissa was still amazed at the size and grandeur of Bret's home. It was a far cry from the modest vicarage where she'd been raised. The dining-room was huge, with a table in the centre that could easily seat twelve. The silver displayed in the cabinet shone in the sunlight from the tall windows, the crystal chandelier sparkled and shimmered, throwing rainbow colours around the room.

The meal was light yet filling. Melissa scarcely noticed what she was eating, however; she was too busy learning all she could about Bret Terrell.

He was relaxed today, easily entertaining her with stories about the history of Salzburg, and the role of the early church. He spoke to her about his sisters and their families, and his mother, all in England. His father, he mentioned, was dead.

About his wife he said nothing.

He wanted to linger over coffee when the meal ended, but Melissa urged him upstairs, conscious of a small boy waiting, and how endless time could be for a small child.

The nursery was bright and cheery, with large windows that overlooked the forest and admitted lots of light and sunshine. By the number of toys, books and games on the shelves, it was obvious that Bret denied his son nothing.

Melissa followed Max around the room to admire all his possessions. He proudly explained from whom he'd received toys, and which ones were his favourite. Bret watched from the door, enjoying the sight of Melissa as she bent over to examine something, her jeans like a second skin, enjoying her soft voice as she admired Max's toys and books.

When the tour was complete, Melissa asked what Max would like to do. He suggested a game.

'I don't know the game, but you can teach me. Do you know it, Bret?' she asked, determined to drag him into it as well.

'Sure, I played as a child.' He moved slowly into the room, amusement in his eyes. Glancing at the small furniture, he shook his head. 'I don't think the chairs will support my weight, or yours either, come to that.'

'Well, I don't either, so we'll play on the floor to do it right,' she said, reaching down to untie her shoes. 'You don't mind if I take off my shoes, do you? If I'm going to be crawling around and sitting on the floor, it'll be more comfortable.'

'Can I, too?' Max asked, sparkling with excitement.

'Sure. Your dad must, too, so we'll all be comfortable.' Melissa challenged Bret, watching to see what he'd do. In the office he was so formal, correct, and in command. At home did he relax and just enjoy himself?

'I can't be the only one in shoes, I take it,' he said good-naturedly, slipping off his shoes.

Bret sat Indian fashion opposite Max and began setting up the board pieces. Melissa sat to his left, stretching out one leg, until her foot just touched Bret's thigh. With a look of utter innocence, Melissa slowly caressed his thigh with her toes.

Bret ignored her as he concentrated on the game pieces, but Melissa could see the muscles in his cheek jerk as he clenched his jaw. Smiling serenely, she turned her attention to the board. She was playing with fire, but felt safe and secure in the nursery with Max. And she always liked to have fun. It would be fun to tease Bret.

As Max began to explain the game to Melissa, Bret sat up and casually dropped his hand by his thigh, reaching for Melissa's foot and massaging it through the soft cotton socks she wore. Melissa felt his touch all the way through her and suddenly found it difficult to breathe. Trying to concentrate on what Max was saying was impossible; all she could do was focus on the exquisite touch of Bret, the strange desires and longings that rose from his caress. Who would have thought her foot to be an erogenous place? Or that the touch of a man she'd just met would fill her with such yearnings?

He leaned forward to point out something on the board, and his hand slipped further up her jeans to touch the silky skin of her calf. She drew a deep breath, moving her foot. This was too dangerous. She would forget where they were in another minute. How could he do that when they were with Max?

He held her long enough for her to know she couldn't move away if she wanted to. Then, with a final squeeze, he released her. His eyes were mocking as he looked at her.

'Do you think you understand the game now?' he asked.

'Yes.' Was that breathless voice hers? And which game did she understand? The one Max was explaining, or the deeper one that Bret wanted? She understood that one only too well. Could she play it his way?

Max was in heaven. He was excited and pleased to have the two adults play with him. His childish chatter during the game gave Melissa some breathing space. Now if only his father would behave the day would be perfect.

Bret used Max's game to pursue his own. Every chance he got he touched Melissa. His hand would brush hers as she finished her turn. When she had a successful move, he'd pat her knee in congratulations. When she didn't he'd squeeze her leg in consolation. Every time he touched her she forgot about the game, lost her concentration. Electricity seemed to flow from him through her, igniting flames of longing and desire. He was slowly driving her crazy! And he knew it.

Whenever she looked his way, her eyes caught his. He was laughing at her, but smouldering deep in his gaze was desire held in check. It was dangerous and exciting. Melissa couldn't believe Max couldn't feel the tension between them. She could almost touch it!

'I won! I won!' Max exclaimed happily as his piece moved to the winner's circle.

Melissa smiled at his happiness, turning to share her delight in the little boy with Bret. He was looking at her again, but the amusement was gone from his gaze; it was frankly sexual, sensual, passionate. She was playing with fire.

'Aunt Sally says I'm a good game player. She plays with my cousins. If I had a mother she'd play with me,' Max said, gathering up the game pieces.

Melissa turned to look at him, frowning at the sudden change of atmosphere.

'I'm sure she would,' she said, wondering for the first

time how Max had taken his mother's death. How long ago had she died? Did he remember her at all?

'My mother's dead,' he went on forlornly, looking up at Melissa's sympathetic face. 'But she loved me,' he said almost defiantly, looking at his father.

'I'm sure she did; you're very lovable,' Melissa responded, flicking a quick look at Bret. His face was still, as if carved from granite. His eyes were hooded and he avoided Max's gaze.

'Aunt Sally says Dad should marry again and have more children so I wouldn't be an only child. I have four cousins at Aunt Sally's and they have so much fun.'

'Max. . .' Bret began, but Melissa shot out her hand and placed it on his knee to stop him.

'I know what you mean. I was an only child, too. I longed for brothers and sisters, but there is only me. It is lonely sometimes. But if you have your cousins, you have family. I didn't even have cousins.'

'I'd rather have a mother,' he said seriously, as if making a great pronouncement. 'My cousins live in England and I don't get to see them often. A mother would live here with me and Dad.'

'Max, since the game is over, maybe you'd like to show Melissa the garden,' Bret said, rising effortlessly. He reached down to help Melissa up, but gone was the flirtatious man of the afternoon. Tension and something else radiated from Bret and he quickly dropped Melissa's hands to find and don his shoes. Putting distance between them.

'I'd love to see the garden,' Melissa said softly as she also donned her shoes. Why was Bret so upset? It was only normal that a small boy would want a mother. Bret should explain why that wasn't possible right now.

Max glanced uncertainly back and forth at the adults

as he packed up the game and put it neatly away. He knew something was wrong but not what.

Melissa spent the rest of the afternoon trying to show Max how much she enjoyed being with him. They laughed and made up stories about the flowers and statues in the garden. Bret went with them, but didn't join in the nonsense. Trying to ignore his dampening presence, Melissa devoted her attention to Max, playing with him until she was exhausted by the time he suggested they return to the nursery.

Sharing a light supper with Max wound up the day. As she ate the last of her sweet, Melissa wondered if she could leave now. The atmosphere had been strained ever since Max had mentioned his mother. She was tired and wanted to go back to her *Pension* to escape the undercurrents of the Terrell household.

Bidding Max goodnight, she followed Bret out and down the wide stairs.

'I should be leaving now. Shall I call a cab?' she said as he paused on the bottom step. It gave her some advantage. Standing there she was even with Bret, could look him eye to eye.

He turned, raising one eyebrow in surprise. 'What about hugs and kisses?' he asked as he moved to stand near her, his eyes level with hers, his gaze roaming across her face, settling on her lips.

'Really, Bret, after the touch-me-not stand-offish attitude you displayed all afternoon, I'd think an affectionate, romantic encounter would be the last thing you'd want.'

'Romance has nothing to do with it. It's sex, plain and simple,' he said harshly. He grasped her arm and turned, heading for the study, pulling Melissa along with him.

She tripped down the stair and hurried to keep up

with him, not wanting to fall. His grasp was hard; he was giving her no chance to escape. Melissa felt a touch of fear.

Slamming the door behind them he turned her around to face him.

'I married for love a long time ago. What did I get for it? My love destroyed, my business near ruin and I was almost killed. I don't believe in love and shan't risk it again. I never mentioned love to you. Did I?'

She shook her head, her heart thumping against her breast. He was furious, and she didn't know what to say to stop his anger.

'Did your *friend* from before tell you he loved you?'

Blinking back sudden tears, Melissa nodded. Brian had sworn he loved her. She had believed him.

'So you know there is no dependency in the word. Don't confuse lust for love, Melissa. I want you.'

'No, I can't,' she whispered.

Bret turned away and moved across the room; sitting on the edge of his large desk, he rubbed his hand down the taut material of his jeans, watching her with hooded eyes.

'I swore when Louisa died that I'd never get emotionally involved with another woman. She almost ruined the business, almost killed me. All for her own selfish ends.'

'What happened?' Melissa asked, afraid to move, afraid to stop the flow of bitter words he seemed ready to give her. Afraid of what might happen if he stopped talking altogether and kissed her again.

He looked at Melissa for a long moment, as if making up his mind. Finally he spoke slowly, 'She worked at the company. We met there, fell in love.' His tone was bitter, mocking. 'We were building up the business, and a huge job it was. I was young, she was young and we thought we could conquer the world. But things didn't move fast enough for her. And she didn't like Austria. She wanted to go back to England. She began to talk about selling. It was a small manufacturing firm in those days, not nearly as large as it is now. I refused to sell out or merge with another company.'

He took a deep breath and clenched his fists against his thighs in angry remembrance.

'She fell in with some Germans who were looking to expand. She negotiated a deal that almost finished Austerling Ltd., even spent some of their buy-out money, all without my knowledge. I discovered her treachery on the final day just prior to the time to sign the agreements. If I hadn't found out, she would have sold the voting power of the company. I quickly let the Germans know she no longer had any authority in the company and refused to sign the agreements, but I still had to repay the money she had already spent.'

He stood up and paced to the window, the late afternoon sun sinking slowly behind the house, the shadows long and dark on the lawn.

'She'd spent the money with her lover,' he said in a low, bitter voice. 'That last day we were coming back from the office, arguing all the way. She apprised me of that fact just before she grabbed the wheel, which caused the car to spin out of control and-over the edge. By the time we were found, she was dead.' Without thought his finger came up to trace the scar on his cheek. The only one visible from the accident.

Melissa was horrified at his tale, wondering what other scars he bore, inside. No wonder he was bitter. What an awful woman Louisa must have been. She didn't know what to say. She wished her father were still alive, could talk with Bret. He'd know what to say.

But she didn't. She just stood there, watching him, hurting for him.

'Not all women are like that,' she said softly after long, silent minutes had passed.

'No?' he said mockingly, turning to look at her. 'My sister Margaret married a rich man just to keep from the uncertainty of our situation. She made no bones about it to us that she was marrying for money and security.'

'And your sister Sally? The Aunt Sally that Max talks about so much?'

He shrugged and walked towards her like a panther stalking his prey. When Bret was close enough, he put his hands on her shoulders and held her for his look. His hands were heavy, hot, and sent shivers of awareness throughout Melissa.

'What I feel for you has nothing to do with glorious romantic love. It's lust, pure and simple. You're a beautiful woman, sexy as hell, and you turn me on. That's all there is to it.'

Melissa reached up and cupped his face with her hands, feeling the hard strength of his jaw, the soft lobes of his ears. She felt a growing affection for him, and it startled her.

'It's more than lust.'

'No. Aside from today, which you must admit was not the best of days, you've seen me maybe a total of seven or eight hours. Don't try to romanticise everything, the way women do. Accept what's between us and enjoy it or deny it, whichever you wish. But don't lie to yourself.' His voice was hard and his eyes glittered down at her.

Melissa felt herself drowning in the blue depths, unable to look away. Could he be right? Her one experience at love had proved her own judgement was faulty. Had she learned anything since then? Was it too soon, too fast? Was she only romanticising her physical attraction to him?

Yet her mother had married her Wyoming rancher after only three weeks. She must have known before then that she loved him. Melissa's eyes widened. Could she love Bret? In such a short time? Maybe not, but she was falling fast. Not that it would do her any good—he'd made that perfectly clear. He was not looking for love, didn't trust women and only wanted sex from her. She wouldn't let it hurt. She wouldn't!

'I won't lie to myself or to you,' Melissa said gently, her hands still cupping his face, enjoying touching him, feeling him beneath her fingertips. 'I'm starting to care for you, Bret, and it's not a good thing if you can't care for me in return. I would love to cuddle and kiss with you, but that would lead to something I'm not willing to do.'

'You told me you're saving yourself for love,' he mocked, his hands tightening on her shoulder. 'And I told you I could make you change your mind.'

'Why? To take out your anger on Louisa? I'm not your wife, I didn't hurt you or betray you. Don't punish me for something someone else did!'

He stared down at her for a long time, finally nodding. 'You're right. I'll take you back to your hotel.' Slowly he withdrew his hands, reached up and pulled hers from his face. For a brief moment he caressed the soft skin of her wrists, then released her. 'Come now, before I change my mind.'

It was dark by the time they reached Melissa's *Pension*. When Bret pulled up before it, she turned in her seat.

'All in all, I enjoyed today, Bret,' she said gently, seeing his tight face in the street-light. 'I enjoyed our

ride, and playing with Max. Thank you for having me.'
She longed to say more, but knew it wouldn't make
any difference. He was the way he was and he was not
likely to change. Not on such a short acquaintance.
And she was going home in a few more days.

'I'll see you to your room.'

'It's not necessary.' Melissa leaned over and kissed
him lightly on his cheek. 'I'll see you Monday.'

He caught her close and gave her a searing kiss, his
mouth hard and open against hers, seeking admittance,
plundering against the soft moisture of her mouth,
thrusting against her teeth, her tongue, causing flames
of desire and ecstasy to build within her.

Despite the strong attraction she felt rising, Melissa
remained impassive, held herself rigid against the
emotions that threatened to overwhelm her. She could
not give in to him, or she'd be lost. She knew he
wanted her, but it was not enough, and unless he
offered more she couldn't accept, wouldn't accept.

'Go.' He pushed her away and started the engine.

She scrambled from the car and watched it as it
drove away, tears flooding her eyes, her heart full and
sorrowful. 'Accept those things you cannot change.'
The words her father had once spoken sounded in her
ear as she turned to enter the *Pension*. As they had
years ago when Brian had hurt her so.

She would have to accept what she could not change,
though her heart ached. She was falling in love with a
man who could no longer love.

CHAPTER FIVE

MELISSA arrived at Bret's offices early Monday morning. She was dressed in her normal business suit, and had again pulled her hair back into a tidy French braid. She knew Bret wouldn't like it, but wasn't going to worry about that. He'd made it clear he didn't want to further their relationship; why should she try to please the man?

She'd spent a pleasant Sunday attending services at Salzburg cathedral in the morning, then wandering around Mirabell Gardens on the banks of the Salzach river in the afternoon. She'd wished Bret had accompanied her, but recognised wishful thinking when she saw it and had enjoyed herself despite his absence.

Derek Millan and Gerry Toliver were already in the conference-room when Melissa arrived, in the midst of an excited discussion.

'Melissa, we got the Stanford works in Birmingham!' Gerry called out as soon as he saw her.

'How wonderful!' She hurried over to congratulate her boss. He'd worked hard for that deal and it was finally paying off. As she turned to share the happiness with Gerry he reached over and gave her a big hug. Melissa smiled and looked over his shoulder, right into the hard blue eyes of Bret Terrell.

Instantly she knew he was misinterpreting what he was seeing. Gently she disengaged herself from Gerry's embrace, but by then Bret had gone. As the others from their team joined them in the conference-room, she soon forgot about the moment. They were all sharing in the happines of their boss, and the good fortune of their company.

'This means I'll have to get right back to England. I'll leave you to finish up here, except for the final documents,' Derek said to Melissa as they got ready to get down to business.

'We're almost finished; the final figures and proposal should be done by next week. Then we just have to wait and see what Terrell decides.'

'No problem. I can handle it,' Melissa said with a greater sense of composure in her tone than she felt. Would Bret even want to do business with her?

When Derek explained the situation to him, it was obvious that he was not pleased with the turn of events. He stared coldly at Melissa, then looked back at the older man as if weighing options to argue the arrangement they were proposing.

'Perhaps we should wait until you are ready to resume negotiations yourself,' Bret said to Derek. 'There is no urgency to this deal. I would be happy to wait until you are available again.'

'But equally no need to delay; Melissa can handle things in my place. Most of the preliminary work is completed. We will propose our final offer in another few weeks. I'd rather the negotiations continue now that we are working together so well. Melissa can handle things this end. And I'm only a phone call away.' He smiled at both of them, anxious to get back to England now that the Stanford works deal was about to become a reality.

'Do you need anything from me now, Miss Carmichael?' Bret asked, at his most formal.

'No, Mr Terrell. I will ask if I find I do,' she replied softly, sad that their relationship had become so formal. Where were the carefree moments of playing the game in the nursery, the enjoyment of riding horses through the spectacular Austrian countryside, the kisses they'd shared?

Several times during the day Bret stopped by the conference-room to discuss matters with Karl Müller or Erich Meyer. Each time he'd notice Melissa and frown at her, never speaking. She knew it best to keep the distance between them, but it hurt to have him ignore her.

So she did her best to ignore him, to treat him in a totally professional manner when the occasion called for it, and forget the delightful day spent last Saturday. Her heart ached, however, that he was so close and yet so distant. She longed to turn back the clock, but what would that accomplish? He had been forthright and honest with her—he was only interested in sex. It didn't matter how she felt about him.

'Gerry, have you seen the production report for last year? I had it yesterday, and have lots of notes in the margins.'

'No, did you leave it in the other room?'

'No, I was checking things here.' Melissa frowned as she glanced around the large conference-room table. Papers were scattered in groups, but none was the report she was looking for.

Gerry looked up and carefully put down his pen. 'Isn't this the fourth time something critical has gone missing?'

Melissa nodded. Reports disappeared. Valuable time was wasted looking for them, or having to regenerate them. Twice she'd had to request duplicate reports from England, which delayed the negotiation process another day.

Was someone trying to sabotage their efforts? The acts were petty, nothing overt. But it was frustrating, and delayed the final proposal. She had a rough draft of what they wanted to offer Bret, but needed to fill in the final numbers and terms. The deal would go forward. What did anyone think would happen by delay?

Joe looked up. 'I think some of our recommendations are being changed before they go in to Terrell.' He shrugged. 'I'm not sure, but from something Erich said yesterday I wonder.'

'Great. Maybe we had better clear the air with our Austerling counterparts.'

Deciding to get everything out in the open, Melissa discussed each incident with her group. Then she met with Karl and Erich to cover the list of all the events that had occurred. She was surprised, and angered, to find the Austrians patronising, minimising her findings.

'These things just take time, Fräulein. Perhaps if you had the years of experience that I do you would realise it. We cannot rush everything. In your zealous desire for success, you see problems that don't exist,' Karl said avuncularly.

'I'm not seeing things that don't exist. It's very strange that these reports and drafts have disappeared, not to be found anywhere,' she said.

'Probably accidentally thrown in the trash,' Erich suggested, trying to keep the peace.

'Then I suggest you change cleaning services,' Melissa bit out, frustrated at her reception. Rising from the table, she left the room and headed toward Bret's office. It was time he knew what was going on.

'Yes?' he replied to her knock.

She opened the door, knowing he would not be happy to see her. He'd avoided her since last weekend, would continue to avoid her until she left if she didn't force the issue. She'd longed for a glimpse of him, however distant. Now she had legitimate business matters to discuss.

'Melissa? What is it?' He rose and waited until she closed the door behind her and took a seat before sinking behind his desk again.

'Bret, do you really want this deal with Larbard Industries?'

He frowned. 'Of course I do; what kind of question is that?'

'Someone here doesn't want it.'

'What are you talking about?' He tossed his pencil on to the desk and leaned forward, his eyes narrowed as he looked at her.

'I'm talking about reports, drafts of agreement language and notes all missing. This has been going on since day one, but it seems to be getting worse. We are not losing the reports. Yet when I discussed it with your managers they blamed it on the cleaning staff. I don't believe them. I think someone at Austerling is trying to delay things, maybe end negotiations,' she said evenly.

'Why in hell would you think that? I direct this firm. I want the deal. The rest of my people go along with my decisions. Karl mentioned that he thought you were ill prepared to handle the job. What kind of trouble are you trying to raise?'

She couldn't believe what he was saying. He didn't give her any credence, but thought she was causing trouble?

Standing in anger, she leaned over his desk, her hands braced against its smooth surface, her eyes hot and angry.

'Let me tell you, Bret Terrell, I'm not causing any trouble unless it's brought to me. But I won't put up with deliberate wasting of my time and that of the

people from Larbard Industries. If you do not want a
mutually beneficial deal between our two companies,
say so right now. Otherwise I'll take steps to make sure
nothing gets misplaced again. And they may not suit
your lofty managers.'

'Like what?' He leaned back in his chair, his eyes
alert, his body poised as if his store of energy was
temporarily leashed and could explode at any moment.

'Like sign out every scrap of paper as it is looked at,
and sign back in when returned. If anything were
missing, we'd know the perpetrator. And start daily
meetings to review where we stand, so everyone hears
the same story at the same time.' It was proving more
difficult than she'd suspected to voice her suspicions.
He was not being receptive. Was it because she was
telling him? Would he react to Mr Millan the same
way?

'I'll talk to my managers. Don't threaten me,
Melissa.'

'I'm not threatening anyone, but I will do my job to
the best of my ability. My loyalties are to my firm!'

'And what do you get out of this deal?' he asked
silkily.

'The satisfaction of a job well done.' Melissa straightened up and moved towards the door. 'I expect the
disappearance of papers to stop.'

She wanted to slam the door behind her, but knew
that would only give Bret the knowledge that he'd got
to her with his nasty crack. She was not his wife, and
he would do well to remember that. She worked for
Larbard Industries and drew a salary. She had nothing
to gain or lose however this deal went, except pride in
a job well done if it succeeded.

Melissa was the last of her group to leave that
afternoon. She picked up her briefcase and scanned

the conference-room one last time. She had checked all the reports on the table. They were stacked in the centre, and there was no way the cleaning people could mistakenly throw anything away. If reports were missing tomorrow, she'd know for sure that someone was deliberately taking them.

She was walking across the marbled lobby long after everyone else had left when a security guard stopped her.

'Excuse me, Fräulein Carmichael?'

'Yes.' She spoke German, curious as to how he knew her name, why he stopped her.

'Herr Terrell asked for you to wait here for him. He is on his way down.'

The guard escorted her to the side of the lobby and Melissa sat on one of the hard marble benches that lined the wall. She was tired and didn't want more sparring with Bret. She planned a nice soak in the tub and an early night. Things would be better in the morning.

The lift doors opened and Bret stepped out. Sweeping the lobby with his gaze, he found her and walked across the marble floor, his face hard and angry, his eyes never leaving hers.

Melissa couldn't understand the look on his face. She sat up, wondering what was wrong.

'May I see inside your briefcase?' he asked as he drew to a stop before her.

'My briefcase?' Melissa was conscious of the guard standing alertly at her side as Bret towered over her. What was wrong? And why did he want to see inside her briefcase?

'I believe I can shed some light on the missing reports.' Bret's voice was hard, cold.

Melissa felt a wave of fear sweep through her. 'Bret, are you suggesting I'm taking the reports?'

'If I might just look into your briefcase, perhaps we'll know, won't we?'

'Fine. Look all you want.' She snapped it open and threw up the lid.

Bret picked up the top folder, one on the recent acquisitions of Larbard Industries that Melissa had brought from England and not yet needed. Below that there were three red folders, 'CONFIDENTIAL' clearly stamped on them in bold letters.

Suddenly she felt faint. Those were not her folders. They were from Austerling Ltd. Melissa looked at Bret, and her heart dropped. He thought she was taking the reports!

'Bret, I don't know. . .'

'Shut up!' He snapped the case closed and picked it up from her lap, at the same time reaching for her arm. 'Come with me. That's all, Konrad; thank you for detaining her.'

Bret led the way to the parking area.

'Bret, listen to me. I didn't take those folders. I don't know how they got in my briefcase.' Melissa protested her innocence all the way to his car, but he didn't pay a bit of attention to her. She could feel the anger in him, by the tightness of his grip, by the way his face looked, the rigid hold he kept on his body.

He thrust her into the car and locked the door. Joining her a moment later, he started the engine and quickly drove towards his home.

'Bret?'

'Do not speak to me now. I'll discuss the entire situation with you once we are at my home, for the sake of the negotiations. If no one else knows of this, we can still salvage the deal.'

Melissa fell silent, considering and discarding ideas of how the folders had got into her case. Was it simply mistaken identity? Had someone with a case similar to hers who worked at Austerling Ltd placed them there to do work on at home? Or had they been in a pile that she'd accidentally picked up? No, she had added nothing to her case in the last couple of days. And the red folders were distinctive. Surely she would have noticed them if she'd had them for any length of time.

The only other explanation was that someone else had deliberately put them in her briefcase. But who? And why? To discredit her? To stop the negotiations?

It was like a nightmare that Melissa couldn't wake up from.

'Bret. . .'

'Not until we're at my home.' He was angry. His knuckles were white with pressure as he gripped the steering-wheel. The muscle in his cheek jerked with tension as he held himself still, controlling the anger that threatened to spill over.

Melissa's thoughts spun. Who could have done such a thing? And how could Bret think for a moment she'd take his confidential information? She knew he didn't have a lot of respect for women in business since Louisa had tried to sell control of his company behind his back, but he couldn't really believe she would steal anything, or do anything unethical.

The sun was setting behind his house as they drew up before it. The mellow stone building looked solid and welcoming as Melissa stared at it with unseeing eyes. Bret had to listen to her. Together maybe they could figure out who was trying to sabotage the negotiations.

He snapped open his door and pulled out her briefcase. Coming around the car, he opened her door and nodded towards the house. Head held high, Melissa walked calmly towards the front door, feeling as if she was on the way to her own hanging. Why was she always feeling this way around Bret?

When they reached Bret's study, he closed the door and locked it with a firm click. Withdrawing the key, he dropped it into his pocket, his face impassive.

'Bret, I didn't take those folders,' Melissa said, ignoring the small spurt of fear that raced through her at his actions. He was a big man; was he planning some sort of punishment for her supposed transgressions? Physical chastisement?

He moved to his desk and opened her case, withdrawing the three red folders. A quick glance at them and he looked at her accusingly.

'Miss Carmichael, these files have nothing to do with the pending deal between my company and yours. Two of them concern the aborted attempt of the German consortium to take over my company, and the settlement I reached with them. You didn't even know about that until I foolishly told you about it last weekend.'

'I didn't take the folders. I haven't seen them,' she whispered. What if he wouldn't believe her? She moved over towards his desk. Clearing her throat, she spoke in a hurried voice. 'Why would I be interested in old news?'

'Don't try to convince me with your innocence. The terms of this settlement might make a difference to Larbard's offer. You could try to wring some new concessions out of me since I had to make them to another company. But the third folder is much more critical. It has the results of the experimental designs we are now testing in our facility in Innsbruck. A very important issue should Larbard try to include this in the deal we are working on. A part of the business I want kept separate from Larbard.'

'Bret, I did not take those folders. I came to you just this morning to tell you we had reports missing. And I'm not sure all the facts are being given to you accurately.'

'Clever of you — to let me know of a problem that no one else has mentioned, so that if something else turned up missing I would search elsewhere.'

'No!'

'Except I know something of how women can work in business. Of how underhanded and back-stabbing they are.'

'You're wrong.' She sank into the chair that faced his desk, her denial falling on deaf ears. He'd made up his mind and nothing she could say would change it. She'd been tried and judged and condemmed, based on what Louisa had done to him so many years ago.

And based on the damaging evidence before her. She knew she hadn't taken those folders. But he wasn't listening to her. How had they got into her briefcase?

'I could call the police. I'm sure they'd be interested in catching a thief,' he said as he sat behind his desk, his face a mask of bitterness and anger.

'No! I didn't take the folders! Anyway, why would the police be interested? We're talking about a few sheets of paper.'

'We are talking about proprietary information that is quite valuable. To sell it to my competition would bring several thousands of dollars. I think that would qualify as theft.'

'I didn't take the folders!' She banged her hand on the desk.

'Perhaps I should just call Millan and tell him the

deal between the two companies is off.' Bret spoke the words thoughtfully, ignoring her outburst. 'And why.'

Melissa groaned softly. 'No. We've all worked so hard for this deal; don't blow it, Bret. Listen to me, please.'

'Very well. Explain.'

'I can't explain. *I don't know*. But somehow someone put those folders in my case.'

'Who?'

'I don't know. Who has access to the files where they are stored?'

'They are stored in the central files, the same bank of files you and your people have been using since the day you arrived. The confidential files were to be locked; obviously something happened today and you made the most of an unexpected opportunity.'

'No!'

'Excuse me, you were explaining.'

Melissa almost hated him as his sarcasm washed over her. He was not giving her a true chance to explain. He believed she had taken the folders for her own purposes.

How could she have ever thought she was falling in love with the man? Granted he was physically handsome, but his mind was bitter and twisted by the events of his marriage. It coloured how he viewed everything. For a brief time last Saturday she'd been happy with him. But he did not want what she had to offer. Now he would not even believe her when she told the truth.

'I think you see the opportunity to make a major difference to the agreement between our two companies, going home as some sort of heroine, doing what Millan couldn't do. You wanted as much information as you could find to hold me to ransom, and you knew just where to look after our talk last week. I don't know how the file cabinet came to be unlocked, but I think you made the most of the opportunity that came your way. Was that why you made that song and dance this morning—so I'd never think to look at you as the person causing trouble?'

Melissa tightened her lips and glared at him. There appeared to be nothing she could say to convince him otherwise. Unless she found out who had put the folders in her briefcase, and how, she couldn't make him listen to her. It had to be the same person who was taking the reports, but *who was it*? Not one of her group, on that she would swear. But who in Bret's group would try to delay the deal? Maybe succeed in stopping it, if this discovery put an end to it?

Standing, she moved towards the window, afraid for the first time that she might not be able to make anyone believe her. She shivered a little. What if he called the police and they took her to gaol, or he called Mr Millan and convinced him she'd done such a thing? Derek Millan was the epitome of integrity. Even if he didn't believe she'd done it, without full exoneration, he wouldn't put up with the implied blemish on her record. Her job would be finished, and the stigma of the accusation would follow her. She would have a difficult time obtaining another post. She shuddered as the full impact of the situation hit her.

A sudden thought sprang to mind. She turned to face him, hoping her expression was as impassive as his. She would not give him the satisfaction of knowing how nervous she really was.

'Bret, who told you I had the folders in my briefcase? Whoever it was had to be the person who put them there.'

He pulled a piece of paper from his jacket pocket and tossed it on the desk. 'I found this note on my desk

when I returned this afternoon. It is a memo from
Erich Meyer reporting the missing reports, as you said,
but he suggests the reports are being systematically
taken by the English group. Under the direction of
Fräulein Carmichael. Erich knew nothing of the
German deal; he started with me after that was com-
pleted. He had no reason to plant files in your case,
Melissa.'

Melissa moved back to the desk and picked up the
note. Dispirited, she tossed it back.

'I was directing nothing like that.'

'So you say.'

'I'm not lying, if that's what you are implying!' she
said hotly.

'Shall we let the police decide? Or your boss
perhaps?'

'Do whatever you damn well want to do, Mr Terrell.'
She'd call the British Embassy as soon as she could get
to a phone. She was innocent and they had better listen
to her there and do something to convince this stubborn
man that she hadn't taken his files.

'There is a third alternative,' he said from his chair,
watching her from beneath hooded eyelids.

'What's that?' Melissa asked dully. She was trying to
think when someone could have put the folders in her
briefcase. Several times during the day, actually. She'd
been out of the conference-room several times.

'You could marry me.'

The world spun slightly, then settled down. Melissa
stared at him in disbelief. She sank down in the chair,
her eyes staring wildly into his. Could she have heard
the words she thought he'd said?

For a single moment in time her heart took wing and
soared in happiness. Was this some convoluted way of
proposing? Bring her back here to accuse her of

something, then ask her to marry him. Was he falling in love with her as she was with him?

One look at his face let her know instantly that that was not the case. Nothing of a happy lover appeared on his countenance. He looked angry, brooding and watchful.

Melissa leaned back, puzzled. 'Why would you want to do something like that?'

'A temporary measure only, I assure you. It gives me time to complete the deal with Larbard without revealing to anyone the circumstances regarding your theft of the folders. And to ensure you get nothing out of the deal. As my wife, you'll have to leave Larbard Industries. That removes you from the negotiations, puts paid to any sabotage you had planned.'

She stared at him silently, unable to open her mouth for fear she would scream at him.

'It also saves your being questioned by the police.'

'I didn't take the blasted files!'

He shrugged. 'So you say. The evidence points differently.' His scorn pierced her. He sat silently, watching her. 'You have the choice, which is probably more than I should be giving. I call Millan and get you fired, or call the police with the possibility of a gaol term, or you marry me.'

'Temporary, you say?' Melissa couldn't believe she was sitting here talking to him about marriage. The bright promise of the picnic in the meadow was far away and dimmed. He thought she was capable of theft. And was proposing a temporary marriage to keep her away from the negotiations. It would be simpler just to ask her to leave. Either way, she lost her job. What would she do at the end of the marriage?

'Temporary until the deal is finalised and all agreements signed.'

'It's not worth the effort, Bret. The whole thing should be wrapped up within a few weeks.' God, this was a nightmare.

'No, I think it will take longer than that. If not, so much the better for you.'

'Why are you doing this?'

'That need not concern you. A simple yes or no to the —er—offer is all I need.'

He didn't even pretend it was a proposal. She sighed.

'Well?' His voice was sharp.

'When the deal is complete, we'll have the marriage annulled?' she asked, stalling for time, wanting clarification. Maybe she could take a leave of absence from work. Agree to the proposal until she could get to the bottom of this.

'Yes. When it is complete.'

Melissa stared at him, taken with his steady looks, the steely glare of his blue eyes, the strong, stubborn line of his jaw, the burnished gold of his hair. Again she was reminded of a Norse warrior, used to victory and conquering. Her heart lurched slightly when she thought of being married to him in name only. And for a matter of weeks. Would she survive?

'Can I give you my decision in the morning?' she asked.

Bret let out his breath as if he'd been holding it. 'The morning will be adequate.'

She rose and looked to the door. 'Are you driving me back to Salzburg, or shall I call a cab?'

'Oh, no, Melissa. There is no getting away from me at this juncture. You can stay here tonight. If you need anything, I'm sure Marta can find it for you. If you should choose not to accept the third alternative, you will still be here in the morning for the police.'

CHAPTER SIX

ONCE the bedroom door closed behind her, Melissa kicked off her shoes and wandered over to the bed. She sat on the edge and stared off into space, unable to believe what was happening. It was a nightmare from which she couldn't seem to wake up. How could he think she'd steal important papers from his company? How could he think she'd steal *anything?*

She was still sitting in a daze when Marta knocked a few minutes later. She brought in a tray of soup, cold cuts and a light tart for dessert. A large pot of tea was steaming gently.

Melissa wondered if Marta knew she was being kept prisoner by Bret. Would she approve of her employer's methods, or side with Melissa?

'Here's a nice supper for you.' Marta smiled benignly and placed the tray on a small table near the window. 'I have a clean nightgown for you; Herr Terrell said you were staying unexpectedly.' Marta withdrew a lovely long white nightgown from one of the bureau drawers and laid it across the end of the bed. 'The bath is through that door. I will waken you at seven in the morning. Do you need anything else?'

Melissa started to ask for a cab, but shut her mouth. There was no sense in putting Marta on the spot. Her loyalties were with Bret.

'No. I'll be fine. Thank you for the tray.'

The tempting aroma of the soup beckoned and soon Melissa sat at the small table and ate everything Marta had brought.

The pot of strong tea gave her fortitude and she again reviewed everything she could think of that had happened during the day to see when someone could have slipped the red folders into her briefcase. She'd been gone from the conference-room several times. And her case had not been locked. Anyone could have slipped the folders inside. But had anyone else seen it? Gerry or Joe? She'd ask them first thing in the morning.

She drained her cup, frustration and anger building at her predicament. With the way her luck was running, whoever was doing this was too clever to have been seen. Yet there had to be a way to find out who had put the folders in her case.

Bret couldn't keep her a prisoner. She rose and moved to the door, then eased it open. Peering into the hall, she saw it was empty. Slowly she crept from her room, listening for sounds that would let her know someone was coming. She heard nothing; the house was silent. Had he gone out? Was the way clear?

Melissa tiptoed to the top of the stairs. Pausing there, she looked over the large entrance hall. It was empty, but the door to the study was wide open, its light spilling into the hallway. Bret must be there. She'd be seen if she tried to leave. Biting her lip in indecision, she sighed gently and returned to her room. Maybe later, after everyone had gone to bed, she'd try again.

Resigned to spending the evening at Bret's house, Melissa gave in to the inevitable. A relaxing bath would help pass the time. Carefully locking the bathroom door, she ran a hot bath using the fragrant bubble bath she found and stepped into the warm, silky water. It was heavenly. Just what she needed to calm her nerves and help her get this evening into perspective.

As the bath gradually relaxed her tense muscles, she

considered Bret's proposal. What would it be like to marry him—her breath caught for a moment—to see him every day, and every night? He would come to know she had not stolen anything, and fall in love with her. They would raise Max, and have children of their own.

Her heart sped up. She thought of the alternatives he'd presented; return in disgrace to England, or, worse yet, face arrest in Austria. Neither held any appeal. But should she marry a man with love on only one side?

Love? She rested her head against the back of the tub, slipping as far beneath the warm scented water as she could. She might as well admit it. She loved him! She'd felt his pull of attraction since that first day in the meadow. The hours they'd spent together had been fresh and exciting. She longed to see laughter and happiness back in his face when he looked at her, as when he looked at Max. He brought life and delight to her, she enjoyed being with him. Should she really consider his offer?

When the bath cooled, Melissa climbed out and slipped on the soft cotton gown. Its flowing skirt brushed the floor, the long sleeves tied with ribbons at her wrists, and the high neck would keep away any draughts. She lay on the bed to wait out the hours. Her thoughts still whirling, she fell into a restless sleep.

With a start she came awake, heart pounding. The room was dark, only the faint light from the stars spilled in through the tall windows, the curtains still open to the starry night sky. She sat up. What had wakened her? She searched for her watch, finding it on the bedside table. It was after two. How could she have fallen asleep?

Rising, she moved to her door and leaned her head

against it. She heard nothing, only the rush of blood through her veins. Quickly she got dressed. Holding her shoes, she eased open the door and stepped into the hall. It was dark as pitch. Could she find her way downstairs and outside? She dared not risk a light.

Feeling her way, moving slowly, slowly, she found the top of the stairs. Softly she descended, placing her feet as close to the side by the railing as she could. If any stairs squeaked, she didn't want to find out tonight. She felt the cold tile floor beneath her stockinged feet when she reached the entrance hall. The door should be straight ahead. She strained to see it in the darkness.

When she found it, she stopped long enough to put on her shoes. Then her hands fumbled with the unfamiliar locks. The snap of the bolt sounded like a shot in the night. She stopped and held her breath, straining to hear if it had alerted anyone else. She heard nothing but her own blood pounding in her ears. Slowly she tried the other lock.

It needed a key. Melissa tried the door; it wouldn't open. She tugged and pulled, but knew that other lock held it fast. Damn! She would have to use a window.

She walked slowly across the hall to the door to the study. Entering, she closed it behind her and searched for a light. Flicking the switch, she blinked at the sudden brightness after so long in the dark. Her eyes fell on Bret's desk, and the phone there.

Moving across to it as the idea occurred to her, she sank into Bret's chair and pulled the phone closer. She contacted the operator and asked for the familiar number. It was still early evening in Wyoming.

When the connection was made, Melissa leaned back in the chair, suddenly feeling better just hearing her mother's voice.

'Hi, Mum,' she said, fighting the urge to burst into tears.

'What's up, honey?' Could her mother hear the strain in her voice across the miles?

'I'm in a bit of a jam. I'm not sure what to do.'

'Want to come for a visit and we can talk it over?' her mother asked.

Melissa giggled softly. 'I'm afraid that won't be possible. I have until morning to make up my mind. Oh, Mum, things are in such a mess. Bret's asked me to marry him. But not really.' She wished his offer had been one of love, and not as an alternative to gaol.

'Good God, Melissa, who is Bret? I had no idea you were seeing someone. Isn't it sudden? What do you mean he's asked but not really?'

Melissa could hear her talking to someone else, probably Jason. 'You're a fine one to talk, Mum, about sudden. You met and married Jason in three weeks.'

'Tell me about this Bret.'

'He's English but lives in Austria, a widower with a small child. And he thinks I stole some important papers from his business.' She blinked back tears. She would not give in to them. He was wrong! 'The alternative is he will call the police.'

'Good heavens.'

'He's given me until tomorrow to make up my mind about marrying him. I didn't steal the papers.'

'You didn't have to tell me that. Do you love this man, Melissa?'

She closed her eyes, seeing him before her, his eyes a soft blue, his lips smiling at her, as they had a couple of times since she'd known him. 'I think so.'

'And does he love you?'

'I don't think so.'

'Is this on the rebound from Brian?'

'No, Mum. This is different.' Suddenly she realised she did feel differently about Bret than Brian. Bret was forthright and honest. He didn't love her, he only wanted her. He wasn't playing games with her.

There was further talking in the background and Melissa held on, waiting until Jason and her mother had finished.

'Melissa?' It was Jason.

'Yes, hi.'

'Your mother tells me this Bret has issued an ultimatum for you to marry him and you must give him your answer by tomorrow. Right?'

'That's right.'

'Or?'

'Or he accuses me of stealing some papers from his office. He's threatened me with the police, or at the very least being sent home in disgrace.'

'And you love him?'

'Yes.' Each time she said it reaffirmed the love she felt for Bret.

'Marry him. No man's going to marry a woman he doesn't love, especially if there are reasons why perhaps he shouldn't. Sounds like he's trying to protect you,' Jason said authoritatively.

'He's very angry.'

'Supports my theory. Do we have time to get there for the wedding?'

'I doubt it. I'll let you know. Thanks, Jason.'

'Here's your mother.'

'Are you all right now, honey?' Her mother's concern crossed the wires. Melissa closed her eyes; she could feel her mother right beside her.

'Yes. Thanks, Mum. I'll call again and let you know how things work out.'

When she'd rung off, she sat staring into space for

ages, her hand still on the phone. Bret had said the marriage would be temporary, until the deal was over. They would have it annulled after that. But she would have several weeks. Would that give her a chance to see if it was truly love, if she could get him to love her? If not, they'd part, no harm done. Could she bear that?

'Calling for a cab?' Bret's voice came from the darkness, startling her. Her eyes searched him out, saw him as he entered the study. He wore a short bathrobe, his muscular legs showing beneath the hem. His tawny hair was slightly tousled. Melissa had a sudden urge to run her fingers through it, dropping her eyes in a sudden spurt of amusement as she contemplated his reaction if she did.

She lifted her hand from the receiver and stood up, moving from behind his desk.

'Changed back to street clothes, I see,' he murmured, still blocking the doorway.

She lifted her eyebrows in question.

'When I checked on you a little while ago, you were asleep, wearing my sister's nightgown.' He nodded towards the phone. 'Did you call a cab?'

'No. I called my mother.'

That surprised Bret, she could tell, but he said nothing, just stared at her.

Melissa wanted to stare him down and met his gaze for a long moment. Heat washed through her and her heart raced. Wanting to be closer to him, thinking all the while of what Jason had said, she slowly walked over until she could have touched him had she reached out her hand.

'Why did you call your mother?' he asked at last, staring down at her, his expression closed, enigmatic.

'To tell her I was getting married,' Melissa said, watching him closely for his reaction.

She wasn't disappointed. He jerked back as if he'd been hit, his eyes blazing suddenly with a bright light. His hands reached for her shoulders, pulling her closer as his head ducked down to face hers on her level, his eyes narrowed as he stared at her.

'Are you telling me the truth?'

'I always tell the truth, Bret,' she said emphatically.

'What did your mother say?'

'She asked if she had time to get here for the wedding. I said probably not. I didn't tell her it wasn't worth the trip for a temporary arrangement,' she replied evenly, wanting him to say differently.

Bret stared into her eyes, seeking something that Melissa wasn't sure she was giving him. But she met his gaze steadily, hoping the feelings she had for him didn't show too much. She didn't want him scoffing at her tonight. She felt too vulnerable, especially since he didn't seem to be the slightest bit in love with her, no matter what Jason said.

But Jason was a man. He understood how men thought better than she. At least she hoped he did.

'You were right. We'll be married the day after tomorrow.'

'So soon?' Melissa was startled. She'd thought they would have to wait a few days, at least.

'If I can arrange it. I'll send someone for your things at the *Pension*.'

'I'm perfectly capable. . .'

'No. You'll stay here for the time being.' Bret's expression grew remote. His hands softly squeezed her shoulders.

Melissa stepped closer and tilted her face. She wanted some sign that things would work out. She still wasn't sure she was doing the right thing with this marriage. And she still had to find out who had planted the folders in her case.

'Goodnight.' He dropped his hands and turned away. In only a moment he turned on the light in the entrance hall.

Melissa sighed and started back to her room. One kiss would not have hurt anything, and it would have reassured her a great deal. Maybe this was a mistake. But it was better than disgrace. Wasn't it?

Marta woke her right at seven, entering her room with another tray, which she promptly put on the table by the window. The day promised to be bright and beautiful. Melissa could see the deep blue sky and the rim of mountains from the bed. She smiled in contentment.

When she was bathed and dressed, breakfast finished, she left her room. Surely Bret didn't really mean to keep her prisoner at his house until the wedding. Now that she had promised to marry him, he must know he could trust her.

Wandering downstairs, she saw the closed door to the study, behind which she could hear the soft murmur of voices. She went to the front door; it wasn't locked. Opening it, she stepped outside. The sun was already warming the air from a cloudless blue sky, the dark green trees were sharply silhouetted against the azure sky. In the distance, to the left, she could see the lacy towers of the churches in the old part of Salzburg. A gleaming ribbon of light showed her where the River Salzach flowed. The view from the house was not as perfect as the view from the meadow she'd discovered, but it was still splendid.

She headed for the gardens, where she'd spent the afternoon last Saturday. It seemed as if a lifetime had passed since then. She would have to see Max before she left. Would he be happy to be getting her for his mother? Suddenly Melissa paused. If the marriage was temporary, wouldn't they be getting the little boy's hopes up only to dash them down when she left? Had Bret considered that?

'Melissa!'

She heard the call and reluctantly turned back towards the house. The decision she'd made last night had seemed so right. Now, by light of day, she questioned it. Maybe she should just return to England. Talk to Mr Millan and convince him of her innocence. A temporary marriage wouldn't change things, and she was setting herself up for heartbreak if Bret didn't grow to love her. When she had to leave after living with him for a while, it would be much worse than if she left now.

Bret was standing before the house, watching her as she walked around the corner. He was dressed formally in a dark suit, the dazzling white shirt and blue tie completing the picture of a successful businessman. She wished she had a change of clothes. She felt rumpled wearing yesterday's suit.

'Yes?' Melissa said as she approached.

Bret took her hand in his, surprising her. 'Are you still agreeable to marrying me?'

'Sure, what choice do I have? Return in disgrace to England and lose my job and my livelihood, or fight you in one of your Austrian courts? Compared to those choices, marriage to you is definitely the lesser of all evils. And will be blessedly brief.'

His lips tightened, but his hand was surprisingly gentle. His thumb lightly rubbed the back of her hand, causing little sparks of electricity to ignite longings and yearnings best left alone. Melissa tried to tug her hand away, but he wouldn't release her.

'In order to avoid questions about our sudden decision, I want you to act as if you want this when we are around other people,' Bret said.

'As if I adore you?' she asked sarcastically. That would be easier to do than he imagined.

He reddened slightly and looked away. 'Yes. I don't want any questions or suspicions as to why the sudden marriage.'

'Because of Max?' she asked, wondering about this change. 'Have you even considered what a temporary marriage will do to him? Alway supposing he likes the idea of my becoming his stepmother. After a few weeks we get an annulment and then I'm gone. How's he going to take it?'

'I'll take care of that; it need not concern you now,' Bret said stiffly.

'Very well, I'll be as adoring as I can.' Melissa smiled suddenly. 'But you have to adore me back.' An imp of mischief made her say that.

'I understand,' he said gravely. He turned towards the house, her hand still in his. 'My attorney is inside. I have had him draw up a pre-nuptial agreement. I will not risk everything again on some woman.'

Melissa was startled, then angry. How dared he think she would marry him temporarily and then try to get something from him? Yet if he truly thought she'd taken the papers from his business he probably thought she would try to get something from their brief marriage as well. Suddenly a wave of discouragement swept through her. She shouldn't go through with the wedding. Nothing had changed. Nothing would.

After she'd met Herr Rollard, Bret sat her at his desk and handed her the papers the attorney had prepared. As Melissa read through them, her heart sank. It was a cold, heartless document in which she agreed never to claim a penny from his estate, that she had no holding or interest in his business, and if the marriage ended prior to her death she was entitled to nothing.

She didn't want anything from him. Except perhaps his love. But to see the terms written down in black and white was insulting. And painful. She felt slightly sick reading it, knowing he held her in such contempt.

The marriage wouldn't work. If he was so afraid of what she might do to his life, to his business, they'd never have a chance, Bret would see to that. Tears filled her eyes. She blinked hard to keep them from falling, glad she was bent over the paper and her hair hid her face from him. She never wanted him to know how much this hurt.

Her very stillness alerted him.

'Melissa?'

Without looking up she fumbled for a pen and wrote her name firmly at the bottom of the agreement. As she pushed the document across the table towards Herr Rollard, her eyes met his briefly and she read the sympathy in them through her tears.

'Melissa?' Bret said again.

She rose shakily and moved to the opposite side of the desk from him, walking towards the window, blinking her eyes, trying to get rid of the tears. She longed for the privacy of her room, but he stood between her and the door.

Then his hands were on her, turning her around, his finger tilting her face up towards his. Tears shimmered in her lashes, flooded her eyes and she avoided looking directly at him. Without a word he pulled her against him, his touch comforting and warm. His arms were firm in holding her along the length of his body and

Melissa leaned against him for a moment, wishing things had been so different.

'If you do not need me any more. . .' Herr Rollard said.

'No, thank you, Franz. Take the document with you.' Bret didn't turn around but continued to hold Melissa. She could feel the rumble of his voice in her ear and despite the hurt she relished being in his arms. Relished the feel of his body against hers, the soothing feel of his hands rubbing her back gently, the strength he represented. She would draw on that strength. Never be defeated because of it.

But he didn't want a clinging vine, didn't even want a wife. He wanted to keep his business safe and make sure the negotiations continued. She pushed against him and he released her instantly.

Without looking at Bret, she walked across the room, willing the tears away, hoping she could maintain her control until she reached her room. But on the stairs a sob escaped her. She ran the rest of the way to her room, closing the door behind her and giving way to the tears. She longed for her mother. She wished she could fly to Wyoming and put this entire situation from her mind. Sinking down on the bed, she turned to muffle her weeping in her pillows, thinking her heart would break. She had been hurt by Brian's defection, but this was worse. The tears wouldn't stop. She wondered if her heart would truly break this time. How had things gone so bad in such a short time?

When she stopped crying, she felt drained. Would the nightmare never end? She had no business marrying the man. It was obvious he would never love her. Why was she putting herself into such a situation?

A soft knock sounded on her door. She ignored it,

hoping whoever it was would go away. Instead, the door opened.

'Are you all right?' Bret asked from the doorway.

She nodded and hid her face in her pillow, willing him to leave. She didn't want him to see her with swollen eyes and a blotchy face. Couldn't he just go away and leave her alone?

She heard him cross to the bathroom, the sound of running water.

'Here, Melissa, let me bathe your face.' He sat on the edge of the bed, the mattress sinking beneath his weight, making it hard for Melissa to keep away.

'I'm all right.' Her voice was muffled by the pillow.

He pulled her up and tossed the pillow to the floor. Then the cool rag pressed against her eyes, washed her forehead and her cheeks.

'I have to protect my business, Melissa. I can't take a chance the way I did with Louisa.'

'I know,' she said dully. He thought she had stolen the files, after all. She should have expected something like this. But she hadn't. And even if she had, it would not have been easier. What was wrong with her that she couldn't have men she was attracted to fall in love with her?

He handed her his clean handkerchief and she blew her nose, feeling better, but she didn't want to be so close to him. He'd asked her to pretend to adore him in public. She did not want to have to pretend. She wished they could really be in love, both of them. Then maybe he would trust her and she would never feel this awful hurt again.

'I've made arrangements at the registrar's for us to be married tomorrow morning. Do you want to buy a new dress?'

She thought about it a moment. 'Yes.' She pressed

the cool cloth against her eyes, then dropped the cloth; she couldn't hide forever.

'I'll take you shopping. You won't know where the shops are,' he offered.

'Can I go back to the *Pension* first and change? This is getting sadly rumpled.' She indicated her suit, now a shambles because of lying on the bed.

'Of course. We'll go there first and you can change and pack. Then we'll have lunch at the Restaurant Hohensalzburg at the *Schloss*, where you can see all of Salzburg spread out before you.'

Melissa nodded. 'Fine.' So she was not even to stay the night at the *Pension*. He wasn't letting her out of his sight. Did he think she'd leave, not follow through after she'd said she would?

'Thirty minutes.' He hesitated a moment, then lightly brushed his fingers against her cheek. 'Downstairs in thirty minutes.'

She nodded, refusing to meet his eyes. 'I should call your office and let the Larbard people know I'm not coming in.'

'I have already taken care of that. And told them the reason.'

'What reason?' Had he told everyone she'd stolen the papers?

'Our marriage, of course,' he said, rising.

Melissa watched as he left, her spirits sinking again. At the rate she was going, life would be a constant rollercoaster. When he touched her she was happy, when he referred to the theft he thought her capable of she was as low as she could get. Was this marriage a mistake? She thought it was.

CHAPTER SEVEN

Bret drove them to the Getreidegasse, the main shopping thoroughfare in Salzburg. He was familiar with the boutiques with dresses suitable for a wedding and Melissa found just the dress she wanted at the second shop they visited.

It was a cream-coloured silk dress with a flowing skirt, a high collar and long sleeves. It fitted as if it had been made for her. The price was high, taking a lot of her traveller's cheques, but worth it. She would have to see about transferring over funds from her bank in England, but for the time being she had enough.

Bret insisted on a hat to match, and after several trials they found the one he liked. Melissa began to feel better about the coming wedding with him treating things as if they were almost normal. He was solicitous in the stores, touching her frequently, flirting a little. She blushed recalling one of the saleswomen's comment about young love. If she only knew the real situation.

When they finished shopping, he drove to the *Pension* and parked near by. 'Shall I wait while you change and finish packing before coming for the bags?' he asked.

'Yes. Give me about twenty minutes.' Melissa appreciated his thoughtfulness. More than he could know. She planned to call his office and talk to Gerry Toliver. There was no phone in her bedroom at Bret's house and she'd been trying all morning to get away for a few minutes. Now Bret was providing her with the perfect opportunity.

She got through with no difficulty.

'Melissa, what's going on? Terrell said you two are getting married and we have to carry on here without you,' Gerry greeted her.

'Yes. Sort of. How are things going there today?'

'Same as any day. We should wrap it up soon. Are you really not coming back in?'

'I don't think so. Listen, have any more files gone missing?'

'Not this morning.'

'Gerry, you and the others need to be very careful. I think someone there is trying to stop the negotiations. I had some confidential files planted in my case yesterday. To look as if I stole them. Do you remember seeing anyone around my briefcase yesterday?'

'God, no! Does Bret know?'

She closed her eyes briefly in memory of his anger last night.

'Yes. Um, that's one of the reasons I won't be coming back in.' No need to tell Gerry that the real reason was that Bret wouldn't let her back. Let Gerry think it was her idea.

'But you and the others need to be extra careful. Don't leave your briefcases around where anyone can get to them. I'd take someone with you when going to their files, watch your back.'

'Right-o.'

'Keep track of the reports, watch if any more go missing. Tell Bret, I guess.'

'Who do you suspect?' Gerry asked softly.

'I'm not sure of anyone there. I'll call in a day or so and see how things are going. Maybe we can flush the culprit out.'

'I'll keep my eyes open. Oh, congratulations.'

'Uh? Oh, thank you. I'll be in touch. I'll call Mr Millan and let him know.' She hung up and looked around. There was not much to pack, and a good thing that was, too. Bret would be here in only a few minutes.

Melissa stripped off her limp suit and quickly threw on a silky yellow dress, touched up her make-up and brushed her hair. Flinging her clothes in her suitcase, she swept her make-up and toiletries into her bag. A quick glance around assured her that she had taken all that was hers. Just then he tapped on the door.

'Ready.' She opened the door and stepped back to let him pass, making sure she kept well away. She didn't want to have him brush against her, accuse her of acting adoring when they were not in public. But she couldn't help watching him as he moved easily across to the bed. Even in her high heels he was taller than she. His shoulders were broad, his suit fitted perfectly. But she couldn't help remembering that Saturday when he'd been in jeans. Melissa tried to ignore the electricity that sparked in the air when he was around. Taking a deep breath, she preceded him from the room.

Bret drove his black BMW to the Hohensalzburg *Schloss*, former stronghold of the ruling prince-arch-bishops of Salzburg. Melissa had toured the massive fortress on her brief vacation before starting the project, but had not eaten at the restaurant. Since the *Schloss* rose on the bluff four hundred feet above the Salzach, they had a spectacular view of the river and the city.

Bret obtained a window table, and Melissa was enchanted with the scene before her. She wished she could spend the entire lunch watching the city, and not have to make conversation with Bret. What was there to talk about, after all? He'd made up his mind.

She ordered schnitzel while Bret ordered the grilled pork. When the waiter left, she immediately transferred her attention to the stone buildings and gothic church spires of old Salzburg.

Bret did not disturb her and she tried to ignore him. But she was extremely conscious of his presence across the table. Finally, unable to continue, she flicked a quick glance his way—to clash with his piercing blue eyes.

'The view is beautiful from here,' she said a bit breathlessly.

'Yes, it is.'

For one crazy moment she wondered if he meant her. He had not taken his eyes from her since she'd looked back.

'Have you made all the arrangements?' she asked, seeking a safe topic. She would not bring up the missing files unless he did. As far as she was concerned, until she could prove she had not taken them she could talk until she was blue in the face and he would not listen. She had to reap the harvest of Louisa's treachery.

'Yes. We'll be married in the morning. At ten at the government building. It won't be a religious ceremony.'

'I should think not,' she murmured, wondering what her father would have thought of the whole situation.

'But binding none the less.'

'I know. Temporarily.'

Bret nodded, but remained silent. Just then the waiter returned with the first course and Melissa applied herself to eating and enjoying the view of the city. The sun shone on the Salzach river like sparkling diamonds on the peaceful water. The rich wrought-iron trim and balconies of the old stone buildings gleamed in the ancient city.

They talked very little over lunch and once finished Bret drove Melissa back to his home.

'I must get to the office. I've been gone too long,' he said as he pulled the car to a stop. 'I'll get Marta to carry your bag up.'

'I can manage that just fine by myself, Bret. I assume it's in order for me to call my office in London and explain why I will no longer be working on the negotiations?'

He hesitated, then nodded. 'Be careful what you tell them, however. I will be watching the other members of your group closely. I have taken steps to make sure such an incident doesn't occur again.'

'I wish you had listened to me when I first mentioned it to you yesterday. Maybe I wouldn't be in this situation now,' she grumbled as she stepped out of the car.

His eyes met hers but he said nothing.

Melissa stood on the steps until his car was lost from sight, then hoisted her bag and entered the house. Meeting no one, she crossed the entrance hall to the stairs and went to the room she'd had the night before.

She tried to reach Derek Millan, but he was not in the office, so she had to leave a message. She couldn't explain the situation, only asked him to return her call.

After unpacking, Melissa spent the afternoon with Max, who was delighted to learn she was moving in. The exact details she left to Bret. He could tell his son what he wished. She was growing fond of the little boy, and saw so much of Bret in him that it made her heart ache.

When Marta brought the message that Bret would not be home for dinner, Melissa quickly decided to eat with Max. When it was his bed time, she read him a story, comfortably familiar with his books as they were ones she remembered from her own childhood.

She went to bed after a long soak in a bubble bath. As she towelled herself dry she thought of her wedding on the morrow. She had no family or friends attending. It was certainly different from anything she had ever dreamed about. As if it were happening to someone else. Someone walking in a dream.

Once before she'd planned a wedding, but the man had only been using her to make another woman jealous. It had hurt so much when she'd found out. She had guarded her heart well since then. Until now. What was there about Bret Terrell that made her wonder if she dared hope he would come to love her? He didn't trust her, nor any woman. She'd been distrustful because of Brian's defection, but now wanted more. Would Bret ever change his mind?

If not, the arrangement was only temporary. Once the deal between Larbard Industries and Austerling Ltd. was complete, she would be free to resume her life.

Feeling vaguely dissatisfied with her uncertain future, she climbed into bed and went quickly to sleep.

Happy is the bride that the sun shines on today. The old saying sprang to mind when Melissa awoke the next morning to another beautiful, sunny day. She'd left the curtains open so that she could see the day when she awoke—the mountains ringing the valley, the cloudless blue sky. These were the things she would enjoy about living here. However temporarily.

Rising, she quickly bathed and dressed. It was half-past eight when she was ready; the cream silk dress caressed her skin, her hair waved around her shoulders as Bret liked it. Butterflies fluttered so hard in her

stomach that she wondered if she could eat. Drawing a
deep breath, she made her way downstairs.

Bret was already seated at the table, the remnants of
his breakfast before him. Max was to his left, chatting
excitedly. He was dressed in shorts, shirt and jacket.
His hair was carefully combed and he looked adorable.
Melissa paused for a moment in the doorway, enjoying
the view of the two men who were to become part of
her family today, for however short a time.

'Ah, good morning, Melissa.' Bret rose and nodded
towards her chair. 'You look lovely.' He was wearing a
charcoal-grey suit, snowy white shirt and maroon tie.
She thought he looked splendid.

Her spirits buoyed a little, she sailed into the room,
a sunny smile on her face. 'Good morning, Bret,' she
said rather shyly. With more confidence, she quickly
turned to Max.

'You're all dressed up—going somewhere?'

He giggled and nodded. 'I'm going with you and Dad
to see you get married. Then you'll be my mum.'

Melissa's eyes flew to Bret, questioning.

'I thought it appropriate that he attend.' He seated
her and asked what she would care to eat.

Melissa had known they couldn't keep it from Max;
it would be odd to have her living in the house for
several weeks without mentioning they had been married. But she was surprised that Bret was letting him
come to the ceremony. It made it seem more perma-
nent somehow.

Melissa was further surprised when they reached the
government building to find the members of the
Larbard Industries team in attendance, along with
Marta, Greta, several of the managers from Austerling
Ltd and Herr Rollard.

She turned to Bret. 'I hadn't expected so many people.'

'You should have someone you know attend. Do you mind?' He sounded stiff, polite.

'No, I'm very grateful.' She awkwardly patted his arm, touched that he'd thought of her in the circumstances. He was determined that others would think it a normal wedding. He'd gone to a lot of trouble for her to make the wedding as normal as possible. Why? And why wouldn't he believe her about the files? Or at least give her a fair hearing about it?

Franz Rollard was Bret's best man and Sandra Stomford stood up with Melissa, teasing her gently about the fast romance that none had suspected. Melissa wished she could tell her the truth. In only a few short minutes they were pronounced man and wife. Bret's kiss was cool and brief.

Slightly disappointed, though chiding herself for expecting anything else, Melissa turned to receive the good wishes of her former colleagues and Bret's friends. Max hung on her skirt and when she stooped to his level he threw his arms around her.

'You're my new mum now, right?' he whispered.

'Yes.' She hugged him back, revelling in the feel of his little-boy arms around her neck. But only for the next few weeks, she reminded herself. Oh, Bret, she thought, what have you done? Will we break this little boy's heart when I leave? How could he stand losing a second mother so soon?

Bret had arranged champagne for all and he and Melissa were toasted and fêted before everyone returned to work. Melissa found a moment to slip to the side and talk with Gerry.

'How are things going?' she asked, watching Bret

nervously. His attention was fully occupied with two other guests.

'Fine, though they have really tightened measures for getting any information. If I didn't know better, I'd think he suspects we're the ones deliberately losing the reports. Good thing you two were so close or he might have thought the worse of you for having the folders in your briefcase.'

'Mm.' There was no need to tell him that Bret did think the worst. 'Any idea who is doing this, or why?'

'Nothing concrete. But my money's on Erich or Karl. Both seem to stall and side-step issues every time we raise a point. Not, however, when Bret is in the room. It's not overtly noticeable, but now that I'm watching for things like that I pick up on it. But I don't understand it; they're both highly placed, respected members of the firm. Been there for years; I can't imagine them doing something like that.'

'I guess not. I wish I knew why it was happening. Then maybe we could figure out who.' She glanced at Bret again, meeting his angry gaze. He excused himself from the two guests and moved across the small room towards her like a wolf on the prowl. Melissa took a quick sip of her champagne, unable to tear her eyes away from his narrowed gaze as he approached. Why was he angry?

'Mr Toliver,' Bret said blandly as he joined them, his eyes never leaving Melissa's.

'Congratulations, Terrell, you've got a fine woman; we're going to miss her.'

'I'm sure you are. I hope you weren't talking shop at our wedding.' His voice was like steel as he turned to face the younger man.

Gerry was not intimidated. With a quick wink at Melissa, he said easily, 'No indeed; we were talking about Melissa's happy married life, and the changes living in Salzburg will bring. I assume you will not be returning to the office today?'

Melissa felt the heat rise in her cheeks. She couldn't look at Bret, nor Gerry. She studied the champagne, watching the slow rise of bubbles, wishing she could sink through the floor.

Bret's arm came around her waist and drew her into his side. 'No. Do you blame me?'

Cheeks scarlet now, Melissa resented his implication.

His finger trailed along her cheek, his look one of amusement.

When they returned to the house, Bret suggested after a light luncheon that Melissa might like to go riding again. She agreed with quick relief and went to change. On the way up the stairs she thought of the insinuation Bret had made to Gerry and wondered if he'd planned to seduce her. It wasn't disappointment she felt at his suggestion to go riding. *It wasn't*!

It was mid-afternoon by the time they were mounted and turned towards the meadow where Melissa and Bret had first met. The air was cool in the shade of the tall pines and firs, but warm and pleasant once in the sun. They talked of many things, but never about work. Bret told her about his family in England, amusing stories of his childhood, and Melissa talked about growing up in the vicarage. It was a tenuous truce, each making an effort to hold up his or her end of the conversation, each carefully avoiding any controversial subject.

To her surprise, Melissa enjoyed herself. The awkwardness and tension she'd expected was held at bay. Bret was charming and friendly and she relaxed in his company, wishing all their days would be so pleasant.

She dressed for dinner in her wedding-dress. Her hair was brushed and waved around her face, her colour high after the afternoon in the sun. She would make the most of the situation in which she found herself. It was not in her to sulk and be grumpy for long. Life was too much fun and she would find things to keep her going until this time was over.

Max did not attend dinner, which Marta had taken great pains to prepare. Bret was attired in the suit he'd worn to the wedding and Melissa felt almost festive. The table was formally set, with a large candelabra in the centre. The candlelight gave the room a romantic tone, and softened Bret's harsh looks, made him look most approachable.

'I didn't plan a honeymoon trip,' he said when Marta had served the main course.

'I didn't expect it,' she replied. 'Is there anything you want me to do especially?'

'What do you mean?'

'I don't know; that's why I'm asking. Do the flowers, clean your study, whatever. I can't just sit around all day.'

He frowned as if he had not considered that aspect and should have. 'We'll be attending the Salzburg Festival in a few days. I have tickets to several of the symphonies and ballets. We'll probably be asked to parties and I want to reciprocate.'

'That will hardly fill my days, Bret,' she said drily. She'd been working for the last six years, and attending the ballet and opera, as well as entertaining. While she hadn't done so on the scale Bret probably expected, neither was planning an occasional party a full-time job.

'Then you can take care of Max. Greta is getting old, and has had very little time off in the last seven years.

I think I'll send her on a small vacation, if that is OK with you?'

'Fine.' Melissa liked Max; it would be fun to spend time with him. At least until school started again. And she would enjoy the Salzburg Music Festival. She might as well make the best of what she had. It was only temporary. She put down her fork, the meal suddenly tasteless.

Bret invited her for a stroll around the gardens after dinner. Discreet lights were carefully placed to illuminate the pathways, and throw the rest of the garden into mysterious shadows. Melissa was intrigued with the difference at night. It was so quiet, with only the soft whisper of a breeze through the trees. The night sky was sprinkled with bright stars, and the lighting on the paths did nothing to subdue the brilliance of the night sky.

At a curve in the walk, where the light gave a soft glow to the whole area, Bret stopped and reached out for Melissa, drawing her before him, his hands lightly resting on her shoulders.

'Are you all right with this, Melissa?'

She thought about it for a moment, looking deep into his eyes, which were softened by the dim light. Her heart filled with love for this difficult man, and she realised she did feel all right. She didn't know what the future held, but maybe it would be fine. At least this time she knew the score. She wasn't blindly falling in love like before.

'Yes, I guess I am,' she said softly.

When he lowered his head and brushed her lips lightly with his, she was reminded of their kiss in the meadow, the ones in the library. 'Big boys need attention too,' he'd said.

Stepping closer, she raised her arms to encircle his

neck as he pulled her tightly against him, his mouth moving to deepen the kiss, his lips opening hers, his tongue seeking admittance into the moist warmth of her mouth—giving her pleasure, inviting her to explore the hot interior of his own mouth, meeting her more than halfway. Melissa grew weak with pleasure. Her heart pounded heavily against her breast and her breathing grew more and more difficult. Still she didn't want to stop. She loved Bret Terrell, loved his touch against her soft skin, loved his hot kisses, making her aware of her own femininity. She wished they could go on and on and never stop.

But Bret stopped it. He pulled back, breathing raggedly. Melissa leaned against him, afraid she'd sink to the ground on knees that were fast turning to jelly if he didn't hold her up. Her own breathing was fast, erratic. Could he feel her rapid heartbeat?

'I think we should go in while we can,' he said softly in her ear, still holding her body against his, his hands against her back, caressing her in soft circles of pleasure and delight.

Melissa didn't want to move. Ever. But she did. At his words, she straightened and pulled away.

'It has been a long day.' She was glad her voice sounded normal. 'I think I'd like to go to bed now.'

As soon as they reached the entrance hall, Melissa bade Bret a quick goodnight and hurried up the stairs and into her room. After a leisurely bath, she donned the long white cotton nightgown and climbed into the big bed. Turning on her side, she gazed out of the window at the bright star-studded sky. And thought of her wedding-day.

She was almost asleep when she head the click of the door. Rolling on her back, she saw Bret silhouetted momentarily against the light from the hall, then he closed the door.

'Melissa, are you asleep?'

'No.'

He moved to sit on the edge of the bed. He took a deep breath. 'I take it from your response in the garden that my touch is not repulsive to you.'

'No, it's not. But you knew that from before.' Quite the contrary. She held her breath. Was he going to kiss her again?

'Good.' His satisfaction was evident. He stood and Melissa could hear the rustle of cloth. She was startled when he lifted the covers and slid into bed beside her.

With a squeak of surprise, she tried to scoot away from him, to give him more room, but his strong arms found her and pulled her up against him. She braced her hand against his chest. His warm, bare chest. Before she could think his hand swept down her back, across her bottom and down to her legs. She felt the heat of his hand through the thin cotton of the gown, felt the heat transfer from his hand to her body, and suddenly she was awfully warm.

'Bret?'

'Shh.' His hand smoothed the gown on her thigh, firm against her muscles, warming her, warming her. Then his fingers caught the hem and pulled it up, so that his hand had access to her bare skin.

She leaned against him, her face pressed against his shoulder, breathing in the scent of him, the pine from the woods, his tangy aftershave, the purely masculine scent that was his alone.

She couldn't think any more, could only feel his hand against her thigh as he smoothed down, up, then down again. Each time he came up he came higher, until he was brushing her bottom with his fingertips. Melissa closed her eyes, the better to concentrate on the delicious feelings his clever fingers were causing.

Her insides were slowly turning into a liquid heat. She no longer had a stomach, only a puddle of molten femininity that was fast spreading throughout her body. Her breasts were aching, tingling, yearning for his touch. She pressed herself against his chest, trying to assuage that longing.

'Relax, you're too tense,' he whispered.

'I don't feel relaxed,' she whispered back. She felt on the edge of a huge precipice, ready to fly away, or fall head first into a dark chasm.

When his fingers brushed against the soft curls at the apex of her thighs, she gave a gasp, her hold on him tightening. Slipping beneath her gown, his hand brushed against her soft heated skin until he found first one breast then the other, caressing each in turn, bringing her nipples to taut peaks which yearned for more.

'Sit up,' he said, pulling her up a little roughly and yanking the gown over her head.

Melissa felt like a rag doll, no bones to speak of as she complied. Eagerly she leaned against that hard chest, the crisp hair she had yet to see brushing against her sensitised nipples, crushing her breasts as he pulled her tightly against him, his mouth finding hers and beginning an assault more sensuous than the kiss in the garden had been.

Bret brought her fire and heat and infinite yearning that only his touch could satisfy. His hands learned her, then his mouth. His tongue tasted her, caressed her, drove her wild. His lips were hot and wet on her skin as he nibbled her, kissed her, inflamed her, setting every nerve-ending tingling with yearning desire. He touched the pulse at the base of her neck with his tongue, trailed fire as his hot lips moved down her satiny skin to the thrusting nipples of her small breasts. Taking each in his mouth in turn, he sucked them gently, flicking them with his tongue until Melissa thought she would drown in the sensuous pleasure his mouth evoked.

Melissa moved against him in growing desire, her hands learning the hard contours of his body, tangling in his thick hair, rubbing across his strong chest, surprised at his response when she traced his nipples.

She snuggled closer, wanting him with a deep burning need.

When he judged her ready, he gently turned her on her back and spread her legs, pausing only a moment before thrusting into her. He was heavy, hot, and filled her until she thought she would explode with the exquisite sensations he wrought. Moving with him, she tried to pull him closer, get even closer. She was hot, panting now, searching for release as his hands caressed her, his mouth driving conscious thought from her mind.

At last she exploded with white-hot sensations, reaching for more, Bret giving her everything she'd ever wanted, beyond all she'd imagined before.

Bret gave a moan and thrust deeply into her, holding himself utterly still as Melissa cried out with her own joy and release. Then he collapsed upon her, raining soft kisses across her mouth, her cheeks. Feeling the wetness from her tears, he raised his head.

'Did I hurt you?'

'No,' she said sleepily. She was so tired, tired and warm and sated. 'No, it was quite wonderful,' she mumbled before giving in and drifting off to sleep, a small smile on her damp cheeks.

Just before she fell asleep, she heard his voice in her ear.

'There will be no annulment, Melissa.'

CHAPTER EIGHT

WHEN Melissa awoke the next morning she was alone. The pillow beside her showed the indentation of Bret's head, and she stretched slowly, remembering all that had happened in that bed last night.

He had awakened her in the night and made love to her again. The memory of their passionate loving brought a soft smile to her lips. He'd been wonderful, patient, passionate, and ardent. She remembered the blaze of glorious feeling that had invaded her entire body. God, she loved him!

She was in the shower when she remembered the words he'd whispered just as she was falling asleep. There would be no annulment. Of course not, after consumating the marriage so thoroughly. But why? She knew he'd only married her because in his mind that would keep her from sabotaging the deal he was working on. He didn't trust her; nothing had changed. Why make it more difficult to end the marriage? Could Jason be right? Did Bret really love her in spite of his distrust? Did he want theirs to be a real marriage?

She skipped breakfast, it was already after ten, so she decided to visit Max and eat lunch with him at noon. She'd learn his schedule from Greta, then he and she would decide what they wanted to do. She felt at a loose end without the demands of work she was used to. For the time being, however, she would have to make do with the tasks Bret permitted.

The afternoon passed swiftly and as it grew later Melissa's anticipation increased. Bret would be home soon. And she was anxious to see him. Would he greet her with a kiss, and pull her back into the bedroom to make love to her again? Or wait until after dinner? She felt shy and uncertain. Had he been satisfied with her last night? Could she please him?

Melissa and Max were laughing over a silly story she was reading him, sitting together on the floor near one of the tall windows, when Bret flung open the nursery door and stood there, looking at them. At her.

Her heart began beating faster at the sight of him, and she longed to rush to his side and throw her arms around him for his kiss. Instead she merely looked up, unable to keep her face from mirroring her delight at seeing him again.

'Hello,' she said gaily.

He took in the two of them happily enjoying the book and smiled slightly, though the smile did not reach his eyes.

'Hello.' He made no move to come further into the room.

Melissa swallowed her disappointment and kept the smile on her face with effort, the sparkle dying from her eyes.

'Why don't you change and come join us? This story is almost finished, but we could play that game again. Only this time I'm going to win,' she said to Max, tickling him a little, her heart aching that Bret hadn't kissed her, hadn't even seemed glad to see her.

'It's not long until dinner.'

'Have Marta put it back an hour and come spend it with us,' she said, afraid to meet his eyes, her smile easier with Max.

'All right.'

In only ten minutes Bret joined them in the nursery. Melissa and Max had set up the game and he was explaining the rules to her again. She wasn't sure she knew all the moves, but it really didn't matter. She just wanted them to spend some time together. It didn't matter what they did, as long as they enjoyed themselves. And it was much easier to be with Bret if Max was there as a buffer.

As Bret sat on the floor beside Melissa, she smiled and leaned over, kissing him lightly at the corner of his mouth, unable to stop herself, wanting him to kiss her back.

He looked surprised, then grasped her chin in his hand, holding her face for a longer kiss. When his lips released hers, he continued to hold her while his eyes studied the faint colour in her cheeks, a look of satisfaction crossing his face.

'Why did you do that?' Max asked, staring at the adults.

'It's what mums and dads do,' Melissa murmured softly, her eyes clinging to Bret's.

'And sometimes more,' Bret said back, looking pleased as he saw the colour rise in her cheeks.

'Like what?' Max asked innocently.

Melissa giggled and sat back, turning to look at Bret's son. 'Like beat little boys at this game. Is it your turn first?'

She was so aware of Bret only inches away from her that everything else faded. She could remember his body from last night, the strong muscles of his chest, the springing hair that grew there. Blond, she assumed, since he was so fair. But she hadn't seen him. Only her hands had learned him, as if she'd been blind. It was not hot in Austria, so there was no need for him to take his shirt off. But she wished she could find a need. She longed to see the firm body that had brought her so much delight last night. That would again, she hoped.

Melissa smiled at Max earnestly talking to his father when she slipped out to dress for dinner. Later she asked Bret what they had discussed.

'He was telling me about his day. How much fun he had with you. You're not old and tired like Greta. You play with him and go exploring. Just where did you go exploring?' Bret asked, curious.

'Up in the woods behind the stables. We didn't go far. Can Max get a dog?'

'A dog?'

'Sure. A puppy to grow up with him. I think it would be good for him. Give him something to be responsible for and to love.' She was thinking of when she went away. He would take her departure better if he had something else to lavish the love he had bottled up inside. He was an adorable child and Melissa wanted him to grow up happy.

'You don't think he's too young?'

'No.'

'I'll make arrangements this week. Do you have a particular breed in mind?'

'No, just a cute puppy that will play with him. I may not be as old as Greta but neither am I as young as Max.' She chuckled and related one of the funny things he'd said that afternoon.

Dinner was pleasant until Melissa innocently asked, 'And how was your day?'

Bret's face closed instantly as he narrowed his gaze on her, his lips thinning in displeasure. 'None of your business. My work no longer concerns you.'

She felt as if he'd slapped her. Especially after the ease and camaraderie they'd shared since he'd come home.

'I wasn't asking about your work, just how your day went. But I can tell it went poorly, else why would you be so short-tempered and cranky?'

'Cranky? That's for children who don't get enough sleep.'

'It is also for husbands who don't answer their wives civilly when asked an innocuous question.' Melissa tossed her napkin on the table and rose. 'I'd like to be excused.'

Without waiting for his response, she turned and hurried from the room. She paused in the entrance hall wondering if she should go to her room so early, but decided she'd rather not be found by Bret, should the idea even occur to him.

Snatching up a wrap by the door, she hurried out to the stables. Maybe the horses could soothe her. They could distract her so that her angry thoughts couldn't take over. She wandered through the stables looking for Schönfeld, patting the noses of the horses as they leaned over their doors, curious as to who was visiting so late.

Sitting on a bale of hay near the little mare's stall, she wondered if she and Bret would ever reach an understanding. Would Bret ever believe her? His experience with Louisa was too close for him to trust Melissa. Yet she couldn't live with him always thinking she'd stolen the folders and then lied to him. If she could only prove her innocence. Or if he would only believe in her.

She leaned back against the wall. How much longer could the negotiations take? The meetings were scheduled to be completed this week, but because of the delays it might be a little longer. Then time to draw up the contracts, sign them. Surely by the end of the month, mid-September at the latest.

Very well, she'd accept that. And not question him again about work. If he wanted to be that way, she could accommodate him. She'd take great care of Max, act as hostess to his parties and his *adoring* wife in public. But in private she'd strictly leave him alone!

And she'd find out who was behind the files in her briefcase, too, proving to Bret Terrell that she was no thief. Who cared about his old business anyway? Larbard Industries was much bigger and that was where she'd be working once this farce of a marriage ended. Damn it, she was not Louisa!

When Melissa let herself back into the house, she was ready for bed. She started across the entrance hall when Bret called her from the study. Crossing to the door, she glanced down to make sure she'd removed all the hay. She might want to go there again, undisturbed, so didn't want Bret to know where she'd been.

'Yes?'

'We're going to the festival next week. I have tickets for a concert. If you wish to buy a new dress for it, I can drive you to Salzburg tomorrow.'

She nodded. She didn't have anything formal to wear. Even at home she only had one or two dresses. There would not be time to have someone go to her flat and send her the clothes. She'd need to get something, maybe several things, if they would be entertaining.

She turned and started up the stairs. She didn't have a lot of money left. She'd have to stop by a bank tomorrow and see about getting more money. Clothes weren't cheap here and she wanted some nice things if she was to play the part of Bret's wife.

She donned her long nightgown before crawling into bed, remembering how Bret had removed it last night.

She turned off the light and settled down. Would he come to her tonight? She turned to stare at the starry sky, her ears straining to hear the click of her door.

It was after one before Melissa admitted to herself that he wasn't coming. She turned over, hugging herself in disappointment. Had she not pleased him? Had he only wanted one night with her? He had made no mention of her moving into his room and she had not suggested it. Now she was glad she hadn't. How embarrassing if she had brought up the subject only to have him refuse.

Melissa awoke early the next morning and hurried to dress. Today would be the best day for her to shop. Greta was leaving at the end of the week, and after that Melissa would have to take Max with her if she went out when Marta was working.

She frowned at the dark circles beneath her eyes. She'd not slept well, and didn't like the fact that everyone would know it. Everyone being Bret, of course. Make-up helped. And she would not be spending much time with him, she reasoned, just the car ride down. She'd take a cab back after shopping.

He was already eating when she reached the dining-room. Melissa greeted him cheerfully and sank into her place, bending her head slightly as she stirred her coffee.

'Shall I take a cab back?' she asked him as Marta put a plate of eggs and waffles at her place.

'No, I'll drive you back. We can have lunch, if you like.'

She nodded, applying herself to her breakfast. Lunch would be nice. She'd be careful to keep the conversation away from his work, and they'd do.

'Sleep well?' Bret asked, watching her in amusement.

Melissa snapped up at that and stared at him, defiance in her eyes. 'Just fine, thank you. And you?'

'No,' he said gently, 'I was lonely.'

She stared at him. Had he wanted her to move into his room? He hadn't said anything. And nothing had stopped him from coming to her room the other night.

'Bret, I don't understand you,' she said breathlessly, trying to know what to say, trying to guess what he was looking for.

He shook his head. 'Sometimes I don't understand myself. I'll meet you at the car in ten minutes.' With that he rose and calmly left the room, ignoring or unaware of the turmoil he left behind.

He was leaning against the car when Melissa left the house, and he stood up and opened her door. After she was seated, he reached inside to fasten her seatbelt. Leaning over her, he clicked in the buckle and Melissa took in a deep breath, licking her lips nervously. The movement caught his attention and he turned his head. His lips were only inches from hers, his breath mingling with her own. Her eyes were wide, drowning in the warmth of his. Heat from his body enveloped her, warmed her. Slowly she leaned forward until her lips were only millimetres from his.

Bret waited.

Closing her eyes, Melissa leaned across the last little distance, touching his warm lips softly, tasting him, taking charge of the kiss and pressing against him to absorb all the sweetness he gave her. She knew she was starry-eyed and the love she felt for him shone clearly on her face, but she couldn't seem to help herself. His touch was magical, and she felt the enchantment whenever she was near him.

'Maybe I should drive you shopping every day,' he said against her lips, kissing her once more before straightening out of the car and moving to climb in the other door.

Melissa smiled demurely and wondered if she at least should try to make more of their marriage, too uncertain, however, to know what to do.

'I'll drop you at the Getreidegasse. You remember the shops where we looked for your wedding-dress. There are more shops along there that will have what you might want for the festival.'

'Shall I come to the office when I'm ready for lunch?' she asked easily, wondering if she would be able to afford the prices of those shops. Her wedding-dress had cost a bundle.

'No, I told you I don't want you around the company. I'll meet you at the Café Glockenspiel on the Mozartplatz at one. It's not too far from the shops. Think you can find it?'

'Certainly.' She tried to keep the hurt from her voice but was not sure she was successful from the quick look Bret threw her way. She would not hurt his precious business, didn't he know that?

She'd try Gerry again, see if he'd learned anything. She couldn't go on with this hanging over her.

The morning passed quickly as Melissa looked for the perfect dress. She found it quickly, a stunning deep maroon and black, long but with a sexy slit up the side of the skirt. She tried walking in it and it was alluring, tightly fitted in the bodice, with a flaring skirt that brushed the floor, the flash of leg as she walked enticing. She loved it and couldn't wait to see Bret's reaction. Try to resist me in this, she thought as she pirouetted before the mirror. It cost the earth, however.

Arranging to have the dress delivered, she knew she'd have to look for a more inexpensive boutique for any other purchases. At the rate she was going, she'd be flat broke before she could get any more money. And she didn't know how long it would take to transfer money from her bank in England.

She asked directions to a bank and was soon speaking with one of the managers of a large ornate baroque bank on one of the lovely plazas. It took some time, but finally she arranged to pay her rent for another two months, and transfer the balance of her funds to an account she opened with the manager's help.

Surely the deal would be finished by the end of October and she'd be back home. In fact, something had to happen before then or she'd be out of money. She sighed as she walked back out into the sunlight at the plaza. Maybe she'd ask her mother for a loan, just to tide her over.

She still had time before meeting Bret, so Melissa wandered along the streets, exploring. She found quaint little shops selling traditional Austrian loden and alpine-inspired dirndls, wood carvings and copper ceramics. She looked at hand-knit sweaters, woollens from Tyrol, and leather jackets. She gazed longingly at the pastries display at one café, but resolutely moved on. Lunch with Bret would make up for missing the pastries now.

One small boutique on the Residenzplatz carried stylish clothes at a more affordable price. Melissa browsed for several pleasant moments, then found another dress she could use. If they were to attend several parties, she needed more than one dress. Her wedding-dress should stand her in good stead in all but the most formal affairs. This dress would be fine for that. It was a sky-blue, off one shoulder and just skimmed her knees. The material was shot through with silver threads, giving the dress an iridescent gleam as the light caught and reflected.

That was it. Until she got more money, she was not buying another thing.

She arrived at the café just before one. It was popular, most of the tables already taken. The wide, sunny plaza was alive with people wandering around, the beautiful fountain in its centre spraying water that caught the sunlight and sent millions of tiny rainbows cascading down to the pool below. Melissa smiled at the pretty setting, glad that Bret had suggested lunch.

'May I be of assistance?' The head waiter bowed as she paused by the edge of the tables.

'I'm expecting my husband; perhaps I'd better just wait.'

'And he is?' he asked politely.

'Bret Terrell.'

'Ah, yes, Frau Terrell. He has reserved a table for you; if you follow me, I'll show you.'

Melissa was unexpectedly thrilled at being called Frau Terrell. The head waiter was the first to do so, and she felt more married at that moment than any other time. Head held high, she followed him in a twisted path through the tables to one near the edge of the shade. She had a fantastic view of the fountain and the passers-by.

She felt almost guilty to be enjoying herself so much when she should be working. Would be working if someone at Austerling Ltd. hadn't planted those folders in her briefcase and then notified Bret. Was it Erich? But why would he do such a thing? Her smile faded as anger and bewilderment took its place.

'I'll give five schillings to learn what you're thinking about. You've had a dozen different expressions in the last few moments,' Bret said as he pulled out the chair opposite her and sat down.

'Not enough. I come higher than that,' she teased back, happy to see him.

His face hardened at her words and Melissa could have kicked herself. She knew he saw her as a mercenary woman; had she just added to his beliefs? Damn it, she couldn't guard her tongue every moment. He had to take her as she was or not at all. Remembering last night, she guessed he had decided on the not at all.

'You've done it again,' he said, the anger fading from his voice as curiosity replaced it.

'I'm feeling a little guilty to be enjoying myself so much when others are working. But I don't care. I'm here and having a marvellous lunch in the Mozartplatz with a very handsome man. I'm going to enjoy myself!'

'You needn't try flattery, Melissa. It won't change things.'

She tilted her head and studied him for a moment, then dropped her eyes to the menu the waiter had set before her when Bret arrived. Deciding on a light lunch of soup and salad, she waited until Bret finished ordering, then leaned forward.

'You know what? I don't care any more.'

'About what?'

'About what you think. You can go to hell thinking whatever you want and I won't let it bother me any more! I do think you are a gorgeous man and I am having a good time eating outdoors in a plaza in Salzburg. If you want to ruin the experience, do it for yourself; leave me out of the ruin.'

'What are you talking about? I'm not trying to ruin anything.'

'You are, by never believing me. But as I said I won't let it bother me any more. Believe whatever you damn well please.' She tossed her head and leaned back, looking back at the fountain, forcing a smile.

'I'll believe you when you tell the truth. The evidence. . .'

She snapped her head around, held up her hand, stopping him. 'Not another word. You told me not to discuss it. And I shan't until I find out who set me up. Are you free to take me back after lunch?'

'Yes, I'll run you home.' He captured her hand and brought it to his lips, placing a hot kiss in the centre of her palm and covering it with his fingers. For a long moment he held her hand firmly in his; the tingling waves of electricity emanating from him danced up Melissa's arms and made her uncomfortable and closed in with the crowds around them.

Why had he picked this crowded place to do something romantic? Was it just for show for whomever might be watching? Or had he wanted to do it because of her?

Surprisingly, lunch became enjoyable. Melissa started the conversation making up stories about people as they wandered by in the plaza. Bret surprised her by adding to her nonsense until she was giggling at his tall tales. Then he told her about real people he knew, the ones she was likely to meet over the next few weeks at the festival, friends he saw year round. He was never unkind, but had a succinct way of sketching everyone so that Melissa felt she would know them on sight, either through their physical characteristics or through some personality foible.

She flirted with him throughout the meal, delighting in his response when he amusedly tolerated her advances. She became bolder and bolder until he laughed aloud at one of her provocative statements.

'You best watch yourself, Mrs Terrell, or I'll take

you up on your suggestions and then where will you be?' His eyes mocked her as he raked them boldly over her body, back to her eyes.

For a moment Melissa wished he would. Wished he would take the day off and take her back to their meadow and make passionate love to her. She would love to feel free and wild and totally irresponsible for an afternoon, and love to share that with Bret.

Dropping her eyes to the pristine white shirt and silver tie, she tried to envisage his chest without clothing, his whole body naked to the sun. He would be wonderful, she just knew. Her fingers tingled again in remembrance of their wedding night.

Gently his hand cupped her chin and he tilted her face towards him. 'You are doing it again. You have the most expressive face. And you go off on your own somewhere and think so many different things. Each expression chases around. What are you thinking about now?'

'Making love with you in our meadow,' she said brazenly, and burst out laughing at his stunned expression.

'Your teasing will get you in trouble.'

She stood and gathered her purse. Leaning over him to make sure he could smell her perfume, she looked directly into his blue, blue eyes.

'Bret, you're going to miss a lot in life if you can't believe anything I say. In this case I'm missing a lot, too, but so be it. It's only for a few more weeks.'

He stood, throwing a handful of schillings on the table and taking her by the arm, almost marching her from the café. 'I told you the other night that there would be no annulment. Did you not hear me?'

'I heard, but don't understand. It would have been so much easier than divorce.'

His breath hissed as he drew it sharply between his teeth.

'It would serve you right if I called your bluff and took you home right now and straight to bed. I could keep you there until tomorrow and see how you like that!' His tone was angry as he challenged her.

Melissa thought she might like it a lot, if the mood was right. But this angry man was not in the right mood.

'But not in anger, Bret. Never that.'

He had reached his car, and spun her around, pressing her against the door, his body cutting off any means of escape. 'If not anger, then what?'

'Love?' she said hesitantly.

'Don't use that word, Melissa. We both know why you married me; to keep from going home in disgrace, or worse.'

'But why did you marry me?' she asked softly, the confining space a safe harbour with his body protecting her from the rest of the world. She was not afraid of him, only afraid of her own emotions. She loved him, despite his denial.

'Ostensibly to put you on my side in this negotiation. To take you away from the dealings and keep what little confidentiality I can for my business.'

'I don't believe you.'

'Do you know of another reason?'

'No, but I don't believe yours. People don't marry for that reason.'

He reached around her and opened the door. He waited while she entered the car, but did not lean over this time to fasten her seatbelt. He slammed the door and soon slid behind the wheel.

'Believe it,' he snapped out, putting the car in gear and pulling away.

CHAPTER NINE

MELISSA dressed with care for their evening at the Salzburg Musical Festival. She'd heard of the event for years, but never dreamed that one day she'd attend. Tonight's concert was by the Vienna Philharmonic and being performed in the same hall where Mozart once conducted. She shook her head, marvelling at the history in Salzburg. It rivalled London.

Her hair was pinned up on top of her head, with curls cascading down at the back, baring her neck and ears. She wore small pearls in her lobes and a matching pearl necklace given to her by her godmother on her twenty-first birthday. Her make-up was more dramatic, suitable for night-time. The dress was a dream.

She studied herself in the mirror, wondering what Bret's reaction would be. Would he like it? The maroon was flattering to her complexion and her cheeks were rosy without the blusher she'd used. The *décolletage* permitted display of the soft swell of her breasts. The tight bodice outlined her shapely form to perfection. She walked around the room, liking the way a black silk-clad leg flashed provocatively in and out of the slit in the skirt. Twirling, she moved to sit on the chair, making sure modesty was assured.

She was ready.

Grabbing her wrap, she regally glided down the stairs.

Bret was in the entrance hall, speaking to Marta. At the sound of her skirt, he turned and watched her descend.

'Oh, Frau Terrell, you look beautiful!' Marta exclaimed.

'Indeed you do, Melissa,' Bret said, moving to the foot of the stairs. 'Like perfection.'

She smiled at his words, almost convinced he meant them. But she knew it was only because of Marta's presence.

When Marta wished them well and scurried to the back of the house, Bret eyed his wife again.

'You look lovely. But I'm afraid to touch you for fear I'll mess up your make-up.' So saying, he leaned over and kissed her lightly on the side of her neck. His lips trailed down to kiss the top of each breast. His mouth touched lightly against the dark shadow of her cleavage, burning her skin, opening to taste her, tease and tantalise her.

Melissa trembled at the sensations that flooded her. She could scarcely breathe, her body was dissolving into hot liquid and she dropped her wrap to reach for Bret's shoulders for support. She might not remain standing if he kept this up. But she could not voice the words to stop him.

He straightened and took her hands in his, kissing each palm then dropping their clasped hands, holding her arms wide to look at her.

'Do you have a cloak or something to cover your shoulders? It will get cool in the evening air.'

'Yes.' She looked around; there was her wrap; she'd dropped it somehow when he'd kissed her.

He fastened it around her shoulders and rested his forehead against hers. 'Maybe you should keep this on. The other patrons are there to enjoy the concert, not be distracted by your sexy attire.'

She flushed at his words and her eyes softened. If

she could only distract him, she didn't care about the others.

As they started for the door, her skirt parted to reveal her long leg, and Bret drew in his breath sharply.

'A man can only take so much, Melissa,' he said, his eyes glittering.

'Don't you like my dress, Bret?' she asked provocatively, aware that she could reach him on a sensual level at least, revelling in her new-found knowledge. He was not as impervious to her as he liked to make out. Could she use that to her advantage?

The concert hall was crowded when they arrived, the women dressed in colourful dresses, the men handsome in formal wear. Bret saw some friends and soon Melissa was introduced to several other couples. It was warm and she removed her wrap. Bret calmly reached for it and held it over one arm, while the other lightly encircled her waist.

She looked up at him, smiling stiffly. She knew this was just a show for his friends. That she'd agreed to act the adoring wife in public. She longed to give vent to her true feelings and to have him reciprocate her love. But for now the play acting would have to suffice.

The concert was divine, though Melissa was too taken with her emotions concerning Bret to give it her full attention. Once they were seated, in an excellent location, Bret reached for her hand and threaded his fingers through hers. It was unsettling. Waves of feelings flowed from his hand up her arm, through her body, disturbing and distracting. She licked her lips and tried to give way to the music, but she could only feel Bret's touch, and remember their wedding night.

Her memory was too good. She could feel herself blossom with desire. Leaning slightly against Bret, her whole arm conducted the impulses from his. Bret slowly raised her hand, his lips touching each of her fingers, then his tongue played with her index finger, soon drawing it into his mouth where his strong white teeth nipped it lightly.

Melissa faced forward, but her eyes closed in ecstasy. She couldn't hear the music any more, just the blood rushing, pounding through her head, her heart pumping harder and faster. She almost moaned with longing and shifted in her seat slightly to ease the ache he was building deep within her.

They were in the middle of a crowded concert hall, yet it was dark, no one could see them. Why then was Bret kissing her? Surely they didn't have to play their parts now, when no one could see. Melissa opened her lips slightly, the better to breathe.

When the selection ended, Bret released her hand to join in the applause, capturing it as the new concerto began. Anxious to avoid a replay, Melissa pulled their hands down, away from the danger his lips threatened.

With a sudden jolt of awareness, Melissa realised their linked hands were on her skirt, right at the apex of the slit. She felt the back of Bret's fingers gently glide over the silky texture of her stocking, the heat spiralling up her leg to the very heart of her. It was so intimate! His fingers beneath the edge of the skirt, softly, gently, seductively rubbing back and forth, while the music soared and filled the hall, filled Melissa's mind with scenes of romance and love. She could hardly sit still.

As the lights came on at the interval, Bret easily released her hand and turned to her, his eyes dark with emotion.

'Next time we come to a concert I want you to wear gloves and a full skirt. A closed full skirt.' His voice was strained.

Melissa stared at him, her own emotions overwhelming. She glanced at the people around them as they made their way towards the lobby and refreshments. 'I'll wear what I want. Keep your hands to yourself.' Her voice was only a whisper; she didn't want anyone else to hear. She licked her lips nervously.

He leaned forward and Melissa thought he would kiss her; his eyes were fastened on her moist lips.

'You are entirely too enticing. If it wouldn't shock the people of Salzburg, some of them my neighbours and friends, I would take you right where you sit. But the car is near by. Not the most comfortable place, but still. . .'

Her eyes widened in shock even as her heart sped up even more. *He wanted her*!

'Behave yourself!' he growled at her look.

'I am behaving myself. You took my hand. . .' She couldn't even finish as each finger remembered the touch of his lips, his tongue, his teeth. Each tingled to have him repeat his caresses. Her leg burned where his fingers has rubbed, her whole body was still aching with desire and yearnings.

He took her hand again and raised it to his mouth, his kiss hot and wet and hard against her palm. His eyes stared deep into hers as his tongue flicked against her skin and Melissa thought she was drowning in sensation, emotions, in the compelling gaze of Bret's eyes.

'Come.' He stood, her hand still in his. 'We'll get some refreshments and cool down.'

Not sure her legs would support her, Melissa rose shakily and followed him to the lobby.

If Melissa thought she would get a reprieve in the crowd of the lobby, she was mistaken. Bret procured them each a glass of wine, then guided her to a group of friends. She recognised a couple she'd met earlier in the evening. Karl Müller and his wife were also present. She nodded pleasantly, wondering if he could be the man who planted the folders in her briefcase. How awful to suspect everyone connected with Austerling. Suddenly Melissa realised she was no closer to finding out who had planted the files than that first night. She'd meet Gerry tomorrow and devise some plan to find out who was trying to stop the deal. She would not let the person get away with framing her.

When Bret placed his hand on her bare shoulder, near her neck, she almost dropped her wine. She tried to relax, but the touch of his warm fingers, the shivers of awareness and pleasure that pulsed through her when his finger gently traced the soft column of her throat, made that impossible. It was incredible to her that no one else seemed aware of the flames that licked through her, of the havoc Bret was causing to her senses. Surely the electricity he was generating would illuminate the entire hall.

His air of innocence didn't fool her for a second. He knew what he was doing; was doing it deliberately. She wished she could think up a suitable retaliation.

By the time the concert was finished, Melissa was a nervous wreck. All she could think of was having Bret come to her tonight and make love to her as he had on their wedding night. She even considered the car, as he had intimated earlier. Could she wait until they reached their home?

The crowd filled the pavement outside. It took several long minutes in the cool night air for them to reach their car. Melissa walked quietly beside Bret, wondering if he was as tightly wound up as she, wondering if he would continue his caresses once they were alone, or if it had all been for show to his friends and acquaintances. Her heart lurched; she hoped it hadn't been just for show!

Once they reached the car, the traffic was a nightmare; they moved no faster than they had walked.

'I enjoyed meeting your friends,' Melissa said shyly. She had especially liked a couple of the women. Maybe she could start making friends. Or was it worth it for a few weeks?

'We'll have to start entertaining,' he replied, negotiating the car through the revellers.

'I didn't know you counted Karl Müller as a friend, I thought he worked for you,' she said, wondering if she dared mention that she thought he was one of two or three who might have planted the folders.

'Karl has worked for the firm for many years, since he was a young man. Longer than I, even. I consider him a friend, though we don't socialise often.'

She was silent for a long time, staring out at the people walking past, at the cafés in the plazas, at the ornate stone buildings built so long ago.

'Now what are you thinking about?' he asked.

'Karl could be one of the people from your office who planted the folder in my briefcase,' she replied honestly.

'Dammit, Melissa, leave it! I don't understand why you constantly bring it up. It changes nothing.'

She turned on him. 'I bring it up because I didn't do it and I don't like being accused of something I didn't do. I do plenty of things wrong, and accept the responsibility. But this I didn't do. I had no reason to do it, Bret. I gained nothing from it.'

'But Larbard Industries could have. And you worked for them. I image it would have been a promotion at the very least, and maybe a fat bonus as well.'

'You're a closed-minded, stubborn man, Bret

Terrell. Instead of looking for ways I might have benefited, why don't you for one moment, just one, think if I'm telling the truth? See what that does for you!' She flounced back in her seat, arms crossed across her chest, glaring out of the window, all thoughts of a loving night gone as if they'd never been. Right now she didn't care if she never saw him again.

The drive back was strained and when he pulled up before the house, Melissa snapped open her seatbelt and scurried from the car before Bret could get to her door. She hurried into the house and ran for her room. Closing the door quietly so as not to startle Max, she wished she could have slammed it so hard that the house shook.

Her anger was gone by morning. But Bret avoided her over the next two days and Melissa missed him. Even though she hurt at his lack of trust in her, she wanted to be around him. To get him to smile at her, enjoy time with Max. She wondered where he was; had he gone somewhere on business or was he just staying away from her?

They were to attend the ballet tonight. She dressed in her other new dress, the blue one that left her left shoulder and arm bare while looking demure and conservative with its high neckline and long sleeve on the right arm. She fashioned her hair up again and carefully applied make-up, hoping to camouflage the dark circles beneath her eyes. She had not been sleeping as well with Bret gone.

When she was ready, she went to show Max. He'd clamoured for her to come see him before they left, since he'd missed seeing her in her other new gown. She loved the little boy. They'd grown close these last few days and now that she cared for him all the time she'd discovered what a sweet, inquisitive child he was.

'You look beautiful, Mum,' he said shyly, studying her from head to toe.

'Thank you.' She twirled around and laughed at his delight. He clapped his hands.

'Has Dad seen you yet?'

'This very moment,' Bret said from the doorway.

Melissa spun around, her happiness shining through. 'I didn't know you were home yet.'

'Just home. I saw you come here as I was climbing the stairs. Max is right, you look beautiful. But then you always do.'

Melissa was startled by the compliment, smiling shyly at him.

'Are you going to get dressed up, Dad?' Max piped up.

'Yes, I am. Melissa can come with me while I dress.' He reached out and took her bare arm, gently propelling her through the door before him. 'We'll look in on you before we leave,' he promised his son.

Bret escorted Melissa down the hall and drew her into his room. It was the first time she'd entered it and she stared around her curiously. The bed caught her eye immediately. It was massive, dominating one wall. The headboard was dark wood, carved and over six feet tall. But the rest of the bed was large, so as not to be overpowered by the headboard. She looked at Bret and back at the bed. He'd need a big bed to be comfortable.

The other furnishings were old, strong and masculine. The entire room was masculine, from the navy drapes at the windows to the rich chocolate-brown quilt on the bed. She saw no traces of a woman. Had he removed all signs of Louisa after her death?

'Louisa and I never shared this room,' Bret said as

he watched Melissa study the room. Her eyes met his in surprise. Could he read her mind now, too?

'We shared the room opposite yours. I moved in here after her death.' His eyes traced down her face to the neckline of the dress and the bare shoulder gleaming in the soft light.

'I haven't seen you for a couple of days,' Melissa said for something to say. She felt as if she was caught in the spell of Bret's eyes.

'Business trip.' He moved away and shrugged off his jacket. Dropping it on the edge of the bed, he yanked off his tie and threw it down on top of the jacket. Melissa watched, mesmerised. She licked her lips. Was she to stay here while he undressed, while he dressed for the ballet?

As he unbuttoned his shirt, she leaned back against the door; she wasn't sure how long her knees would hold her up. She couldn't take her eyes off him.

Bret ran his hand over his cheek and chin and glanced over at Melissa. 'Come talk to me while I shave.' He went into the bathroom, shrugging out of his shirt and tossing it into a big laundry basket along one wall.

Melissa moved slowly across the room to the door of the large bathroom. Bret was already running water, lathering his face. She paused at the door and feasted her gaze on him. Clearly defined shoulder muscles rippled beneath his skin as he moved to lather his face and begin shaving. In the mirror she could see the mat of hair that covered his chest, the dark nipples nestled in the blond curls. Her fingers ached to touch him, tangle in the hair she remembered from their wedding night, feel him against her again, her hands on his hot skin, tracing the muscles that moved so enticingly.

Bret caught her eye in the mirror, his narrowed and

considering. 'So what were you and Max up to while I was gone?'

'Where were you?' She took a step closer, still staring at him in the mirror. He was gorgeous. How could he manage to live so long and not be aware of the effect he had on women? She'd never seen any evidence of it. Yet he was the best-looking thing she'd ever seen. His belt was open and Melissa's gaze dropped to his waist, then snapped back up to meet his eyes. His smile as he dropped his look to rinse the razor told her he'd noticed where she'd been looking. He looked triumphant, satisfied, all male.

'Business. I had to go to Vienna. Have to go back in a couple of weeks. I would have told you after the concert, but you—er—left rather abruptly. Did you miss me?' he asked lightly, concentrating on shaving his neck, his face tilted away from her.

'Yes,' she said softly. She hadn't lied to him yet; there was no reason to start now. 'But Max and I had fun. We went to Mirabell Gardens yesterday. He loved the little dwarfs and I loved the river walk. Then we ate at a little café and came home.'

It had taken the last of her money, but had been worth it. Max had not been before and had enjoyed the day immensely.

'We could go to Schloss Hellbrunn one day; he'd like that. They have fountains that spray across the walkways. If you're not quick, you get wet,' Bret said, rinsing his face and patting it with some aftershave.

'That'd be fun. Max will start school before long; we should plan it soon.'

He tossed down the towel and moved towards her. Melissa stared at his chest, broad and solid. She licked her lips and raised her gaze to his as he came to stand before her. Her eyes widened slightly before she let her lids drift closed as he leaned over her and kissed her.

His lips were cool against hers. The tangy scent of his aftershave filled her nostrils. He coaxed her into a response and Melissa was lost. She leaned into the kiss, opening her mouth for the pleasure she knew he'd give her. But he held back, moving his lips across hers, back and forth, before finally moving to deepen the kiss with his tongue.

Her mouth became the focal point of her life. The tantalising delights Bret brought with his tongue, his lips, his teeth caught up her very being and she was anchored to earth only by his touch. When he slid the zip down on her dress, she was scarely aware. He eased the dress from her shoulder, pulling it to her waist.

'My God, you're not even wearing a bra!'

'Bret.' She pulled back, her right arm caught at her side by the dress, her left arm free to push against him, to have her fingers tangle in the crisp hair of his chest, tangle and linger. Caress. Stroke.

He looked at her creamy breasts, his hand cupping her, his thumb circling one dark rosy circle, brushing back and forth just beneath the tip of her nipple, causing it to pucker and harden. Melissa gave a soft moan, wanting more, wanting him to touch her the way he had once before, one glorious night.

When she thought she would die with the wanting, he leaned his head over and captured the tortured nipple in his mouth. The hot wetness was wonderful. Melissa reached behind his head to hold him against her as his arm moved against her back to bring her hard against him. She gave a soft groan, feeling the hot liquid in the centre of her being, now focused on his touch at her breast. When he suckled gently, she felt as if she would collapse in a puddle of molten sensation and sensual pleasure. She was panting with desire, longing. Her hips moved in a seeking gesture, the yearning building to fever pitch. God, he was burning her up inside.

Bret left the one breast to take the other in his mouth, loving it, laving it, sucking gently until Melissa could stand it no longer.

'Bret.' She was almost sinking on the floor. He either had to stop, or she wouldn't be able to stay upright.

Slowly he lifted his head to capture her mouth with his. He was hot and wet and pulsing with energy. She felt the strength of his chest, his hot skin pressing against hers as his arms tightened, holding her against him, while his mouth continued its invasion at a slow pace.

The knock at the door came unexpectedly.

Melissa froze, slowly pulling back from Bret.

'Herr Terrell? Shall I bring you a little something to eat before you leave?' Marta called.

Bret took a ragged breath and slowly released Melissa. He pushed her into the bathroom and partially closed the door before moving across the room to the bedroom door. Opening it a bit, he spoke to Marta. Melissa couldn't hear what he was saying, and didn't try. She used the time to pull up her dress and zip it closed. Turning to the mirror, she could see her lips were swollen and rosy. Her hair was tousled and her lipstick gone. It wouldn't take too long to repair the damages, if she could walk back to her room. Her legs still felt weak, her whole body yearned for his touch.

When she heard the door close, she left the bathroom, not meeting Bret's eyes. 'I need to fix my face again,' she said, walking towards the door.

'I'll be ready in ten minutes.' Gone was the hot voice that had spoken to her in the bathroom only moments ago. In its place was the cool tones she was used to hearing from him. She blinked against sudden tears that threatened.

The ballet was beautiful and Melissa enjoyed herself. Bret seemed preoccupied and did not torment her as he had at the concert, so she was able to focus on the performance. Afterwards they met for a late supper with some of his friends. Apparently he'd forgotten his request for them to act as if they were passionately in love. He treated her cordially, but almost as if she were the business acquaintance she had once been.

When she was in bed, alone again, disappointment filled her when she realised he wouldn't come to sleep with her. She closed her eyes and relived every moment of their one night together. It only made her yearn for more.

The dinner party resulted in two more invitations to events planned in conjunction with the festival. Melissa knew she'd need another dress, and just didn't have the funds. But Bret accepted for them and she could find no reason to refuse.

She worried about the invitations the next morning. She was distracted when playing with Max, couldn't concentrate when Marta asked her a question, and forgot to call Gerry to find out how the deal was progressing.

Finally Melissa admitted she had to do something; she could no longer expect to be back in England before her funds ran out. She was almost broke now.

Her mother would lend her some money. She hated to call her, to let her know that things weren't going as well as she probably hoped they would be, but no matter. Her mother would stand by her.

The call actually went better than Melissa had expected. The questions were at a minimum, and her mother accepted the vague answers Melissa gave without doubt. But it would still take several days for the money to reach Austria, and Melissa would have to exchange it. Her problem was immediate. She needed to get a new dress by dinner two days hence.

She was still worrying over the problem at dinner that night. Bret seemed content with desultory conversation and Melissa was happy to make only small talk. She knew she'd have to do something soon, or wear her wedding-dress to the dinner party in two day's time.

After dinner, before they left the dining-room, Bret stopped Melissa as she was made to rise from the table.

'Wait. I have something for you.' He drew a long narrow box from his pocket. It was wrapped in silver paper, with a small white bow on top. He handed it to her and watched as she opened it.

Melissa was curious. He'd never given her anything before. What could this be?

A beautiful necklace of diamonds and sapphires glittered up at her as she removed the lid. There were two earrings as well. The fiery rainbow of colours from the diamonds was dazzling, the rich deep blue of the sapphires resplendent on the velvet cushion.

She stared at the gems for a long moment, then snapped closed the box and shoved it across the table at Bret, meeting his eyes, determination rampant in hers.

'Thank you, but I cannot accept.' She rose, ready to leave.

'And why not?' He looked almost disappointed.

'Because I can't.' She looked away, hurt building within her. He had no business tempting her like that.

'Wait a minute.' Bret rose and came round the table to her side. 'Why not? I want you to have them.'

She raised her head proudly and stared back at him, anger now beginning to build, for which she was grateful. She needed it to sustain her.

'Because of that damned agreement you had me sign. I will take nothing from you or your precious estate. A flower is one thing, maybe. But that necklace must have cost a fortune. Never will I have you intimate that I'm mercenary and greedy, in this for what I can get out of it.'

'Melissa, this has nothing to do with the agreement.'

'Oh, no? Do you still think I took the folders?' she demanded, her hands on her hips as she leaned towards him, her eyes blazing.

He glanced at the necklace. 'This has nothing to do with the folders either. I wanted you to have it to wear with some of your dresses. It would look beautiful with the one you wore last night.' His eyes avoided hers, and his stance was rigid, as if he held on to composure by a tenuous thread.

'So it's on loan for when we go out?'

'No, it's for you to have!' His anger flared.

'What happens when I leave? Then I'm accused of taking money from your estate? No, thanks.' She moved to pass him, but he reached out and stopped her.

'It is perfectly acceptable for a husband to give his wife a damned necklace!'

'It's acceptable in a normal marriage, where husbands and wives love each other and support each other and help each other. But not in this farce of a relationship we're in. You don't believe me. A real husband would believe in his wife! Leave me alone!'

She jerked out of his grasp and ran from the room, angered and upset by the whole thing. The necklace was beautiful. She would have given almost anything to have received it with his love. To have him fasten it around her neck and kiss her gently, telling her he loved her.

But he didn't love her and she didn't want anything else from him.

CHAPTER TEN

THE next morning Melissa waited until Bret had left for work before descending the stairs. She was going to Salzburg herself this morning, but didn't want Bret to know what she'd decided to do. In her pocket was her pearl necklace. She hoped she could find a jewellery shop that would give her enough money for her immediate needs, and maybe let her redeem it once the money from her mother arrived.

As she ate breakfast in the lonely dining-room she wondered how much longer it would be before the deal with Larbard Industries would be completed. She had talked to Mr Millan just after the wedding to let him know she was leaving. He'd said he would always find a place for her if she ever wanted to come back to work. Would he be surprised to find her requesting to return after only a month or so of marriage?

She had arranged to meet with Gerry for lunch to discuss the problems they were having and try to determine a way to get to the source of the difficulties. She was growing more and more determined to uncover the true culprit and make sure Bret knew she was not a thief!

The cab dropped her at a small jewellery shop off one of the plazas. Melissa lifted her head as she walked in. There was nothing shameful about falling on hard times. And she would be able to reclaim the necklace in only a few days, once she had the money her mother was sending.

There might be nothing shameful in it, but is was

147

certainly embarrassing, Melissa thought later as she
shut the door behind her and began walking towards
the boutiques on Getreidegasse. The manager had tried
to make the transaction pleasant enough, but she'd felt
a pang when she'd turned over her precious necklace.
He'd assured her that he would not sell it for two
weeks—plenty of time for her to retrieve it should her
funds come through. But she felt he didn't think she
really had any money coming.

It had been awkward when she'd had to give him her
name for the receipt. She only hoped the Terrell name
was common enough that he would not make the
connection with Bret.

She found two dresses that would be suitable for the
dinner parties to which they had been invited. This
would give her four outfits to switch among. She
wouldn't need anything more for her stay here, no
matter how much they entertained.

Gerry was already at the restaurant when she
arrived. They ordered quickly and Gerry drew out a
file folder.

'I've made notes on everything I know of that has
happened. And the order. What do you think?' He slid
the paper across the table.

Melissa read the list of incidents, trying to see a
pattern, trying to see who could be doing this. Gerry
had a couple since she'd left, but nothing concrete
enough to take to Bret. And if they did, would he
continue to think the English group was doing it? Was
he too bitter even to consider someone in his own firm?

'So where do you stand now?' Melissa asked, still
studying the list. Surely there was something, if only
she could see it.

'This has delayed us, of course, but we are just about

ready to submit the final proposal. If Terrell agrees, and signs, it's a done deal.'

Melissa sat back in her chair and looked at Gerry. 'I think I have an idea. It might work, it might not. Can you have a proposal to give to Bret, but not give it to him? Hold it for a day and a night?'

Gerry stared at her, understanding starting to show. 'Sure. I'll wait for a night he's going to be gone, then the packet can arrive that afternoon and be left out overnight. You're thinking the person doing all this will come in that night and take it?'

'That, or alter it. Or at least read it, not wanting to wait until after Bret sees it. What do you think?'

'There's more?'

She nodded, smiling excitedly. 'Sure. I'll be there. When whoever it is sneaks back in after dark, I'll be there to see him or her.'

'No, too dangerous.'

'Why?'

'If someone's been doing all this, they surely don't want to be discovered. Who knows what could happen if you're there alone?'

'Gerry, I have to find out.'

'I'll be there too.'

'No, what if the person watches to see who leaves? I need you to smuggle me in during the day. I'll hide in the Ladies' until after dark, then hide in that little ante-room off the main conference-room. I don't have to let the person know I'm there.'

He considered the plan for a long moment, then nodded. 'OK, Melissa, but I hope you know what you're doing.'

'I want to find out who has been doing this. Who planted those folders in my briefcase.' Her voice was steely in her determination.

She and Gerry finalised their plans, including how he was to notify her when the papers were to be left so she'd know she had to get to the office in the afternoon.

After lunch, she took a cab home, glad to be able to spend the rest of the day with Max. Changing into shorts, they went to explore the forest behind the house. She thought again how much he would enjoy a dog, and would have to remind Bret at the first opportunity.

They were back in the nursery, playing soldiers, when Marta appeared in the open doorway.

'Herr Terrell is in the study, Frau Terrell, and he would like to see you.'

Melissa looked up in surprise. Was something wrong? Bret never came home mid-afternoon. She hurried down the stairs, worried that something had gone wrong at his firm. Or with him.

Bret was standing by the tall windows looking out when Melissa peeked in the opened door.

'Bret?'

When he turned, Melissa could see his anger. Instantly she was reminded of the folders in the briefcase. Her eyes searched his desk. Had something else happened?

'What's wrong?' she asked, crossing the floor slowly, pausing near one of the chairs by his desk, watching him warily. She was conscious of how scruffy she looked in her shorts and brief top compared to his immaculate business suit.

He glared at her for a long moment, then slid his hand into his jacket pocket, withdrawing her pearl necklace. Dangling it from his fingers, he said with deceptive calm, 'Perhaps you would care to give me an explanation about this?'

Melissa sank into the chair, staring at the tell-tale necklace, her head spinning. How had he found out?

'It looks like my necklace,' she said slowly, afraid to meet his eyes.

'I recognised it when Herr Janis brought it to me. You've worn it a couple of times. What I want to know is why he had it in the first place.'

She could hear the suppressed fury in his voice.

'I sold it to him, sort of.'

'But were you planning to buy it back?'

'Yes.'

'When? How?'

She shivered at his tone. 'In a few days. I—er—have some money coming to me then.'

'And how do you have money coming to you? Are you planning some other form of delay on the sale of stock to your company, something besides strong-arm tactics once the terms of the deal with the German firm are known? Something that would get you immediate payment for your part?' Bret's voice was deadly, his eyes glittered in anger.

Melissa stood up to meet his gaze, her own anger rising.

'No! If you must know Mr Distrustful, I'm expecting some money from my mother. Just what do you think I have to live on when I'm not working? Air? You haven't given me one bloody schilling, but still I'm supposed to dress for the elaborate concerts and dinner parties you want to attend. I'm supposed to do you credit and act the adoring wife. I can't very well do it in rags. There's been no time to get my clothes over from England, not that I have that much to wear that would be suitable.'

She took a step towards him, her hands clenched tightly in fists. She was so enraged she would like to hit him! How dared he insult her so? She would not stand for it!

'And not that it's worth the bloody damn trouble to bring anything over here. As soon as the deal is done, I'm leaving!'

Bret reached for her hand and coaxed it open, dropping the necklace in it and closing her fingers around it gently, his hand holding hers.

'Don't swear,' he said softly. 'It's unbecoming in a vicar's daughter. I'm very sorry, Melissa. I have handled this badly. Please forgive me.'

She stared up at him with stunned eyes. He was apologising?

'I don't expect you to use your money to support yourself while you are my wife. Why didn't you say something to me?'

'You're kidding, right?' Melissa said, conscious of his fingers still clasping hers, of the energy that seemed to transfer from his hand to hers. She suddenly wished he'd kiss her.

'No, I'm not.'

'Bret, after that agreement you had me sign, I'm lucky to get dinner,' she said in exasperation.

He stiffened. 'For God's sake, Melissa, that is protection I felt was needed after your attempt to sabotage the negotiations. But it had nothing to do with day-to-day living. Of course you must have money; how do you expect to do anything?'

'I don't expect to be here that long for it to matter,' she shot back. 'And I didn't take the damned folders.'

'Are you so unhappy here?' he asked, drawing her closer, enveloping her in the warmth of his gaze, the warmth of his body as he slowly pulled her into his arms.

Melissa rested against his chest, hearing the steady

beat of his heart beneath her ear. If only she could stay like this forever.

'Every wife likes it when her husband thinks she's a thief and a liar. How could you think me unhappy?'

'I still want you,' he said in a low voice. Tilting her head up, he lowered his until his lips touched hers, flaming into passion, moving persuasively against hers.

Melissa tried to resist. She wanted to resist. She wanted to show him he couldn't affect her at all. But it was a lie. She loved his touch, craved it. A second's resistance was all she could muster. Then she was kissing him back. Delighting in the feel of his mouth on hers, his breath mingling with hers, his heart pounding in time with hers. Her tongue curled around his when he invaded her, and she moaned in sheer pleasure. Would that they could expand that pleasure as they had once before. Would he ever make love to her again?

She moved against him, rubbing her hips against his, thrilled to note his arousal. He was not so impervious to her, she thought. His arms tightened around her and one hand slid down her back to cup her bottom and hold her tightly against him, stopping the rubbing she'd been doing. He grew harder and heat spread throughout her. Heat and desire. She wanted him as much as he wanted her. God, she loved him so much. Couldn't he love her just a little?

'Dad?'

Bret froze, his hand sliding up to the small of her back. Slowly he raised his face, his lips leaving hers. Melissa leaned against him, her face tucked in by his neck, breathing in the scent of him, the scent that was uniquely Bret. Her heart was racing and her breathing erratic.

'Yes, Max?'

She marvelled at his even tone. His arms still held her, but he was now looking at his son standing in the open doorway. She should have closed it behind her when she first came in.

'Is Mum coming back to play with me?' Max asked, his eyes fixed upon his father's.

'Yes. She'll be along in a few minutes. I was just—er—giving her a cuddle.'

Melissa smiled at the strain in his voice. He was obviously not used to explaining things to Max. It was quite endearing. She raised her face to his, hers brimming with amusement, waiting to see how he would handle the situation.

'I like it, too, when Mum cuddles me,' Max said solemnly.

'Who cuddles better?' Bret said so softly that only Melissa heard him, his eyes mocking her.

She pushed back, momentarily sorry when he released her. But if she was to go with Max, she might as well go now. 'About even, I guess,' she said, laughing at his expression.

'Baggage! Wait a moment.' He reached into his trouser pocket and pulled out a sheaf of bills. Peeling off several, he handed them to Melissa.

'This will tide you over in the meantime. Next week we'll go to the bank and get you an account.'

When she hesitated, he said, 'Take the money, Melissa. I don't want another argument.'

She nodded and took the money. 'OK, Bret, but I already opened an account when I transferred my money from England.'

Maybe she could call her mother again and let her know things were better and she wouldn't need her money.

'Dad, would you like to come play with us? We're

playing war. Melissa is telling me about the Armada
and Trafalgar and Napoleon.'

'Armada and Napoleon?'

'I'm condensing things a little,' she said, smiling.
'They are all exciting events to a small boy. He can
learn the proper history later.'

'Yes, I'll come see this, after I change.'

Max beamed at his father, taking Melissa's hand. As
they walked up the stairs, Bret could hear his son's
young voice. 'Things are ever so better here since you
came, Melissa. Dad never came home during the day.
And never played with me except on the weekend.'

The afternoon came alive for Melissa when Bret
joined them. He'd changed to jeans and an old T-shirt.
Barefoot, he mentioned it was easier to be crawling
around without shoes. Melissa agreed, hiding her
delight at his joining them. She suspected that a few
weeks ago he would never have thought of it, finding
work too engrossing. She had long ago discarded her
shoes and had been crawling around on the floor
supporting the attack formations of the soldiers for
ages. But she paused now to study her husband, noting
his muscular chest beneath the shirt, wishing again that
he'd take it off.

Bret played differently than Max. For one thing,
Melissa noticed immediately, he touched her every
chance he got. When her foot was in the way of his
advance, he would move it gently, his hand lingering,
caressing. If she started to move a man before Bret
wanted her to, he'd take her hand, holding it above the
soldier, his fingers moving seductively against her palm.
Twice he deliberately brushed against her breast when
leaning over to move one of his soldiers.

When Melissa's eyes sought his, she would find

gentle amusement, and something else. Could it be desire?

She moved around, the battles furious and fun. Max laughed and Bret watched his son with indulgence. He had never seen him so happy.

Melissa sat down, Indian style, and leaned back against her hands. It was Max's turn for some advancement and she was enjoying his enthusiasm. Bret moved over and sat beside her, his hand casually dropping to rest on her bare thigh, just below her shorts. Her breath stopped, her heart stopped. Melissa felt a curious numbness spread throughout her body, followed immediately by pulsating heat. Bret's fingers gently rubbed against the soft skin of her inner thigh and she could concentrate on nothing else. She longed for him to move his hand upwards, to assuage the growing yearning she felt for his touch. For the ending of the sexual tension he built in her every time he touched her.

Today was endless. And still his hand moved gently, slipping further up, to the edge of her shorts. Could he slip beneath? She couldn't look at him, afraid for him to see the naked longing she knew must be reflected in her eyes. She felt it so strongly that she knew she could never hide it. And especially from Bret. God, he was practically seducing her in front of Max!

'Your turn Dad,' Max said, smiling innocently.

'Max, go down to Marta and ask her for some cookies and milk. We'll continue when you get back,' Bret said, his hand still caressing.

When the little boy scrambled to his feet and ran to see about a treat, Bret looked at Melissa. His gaze was hungry with want as he pushed her back on the floor, his hand moving up to the apex of her thighs, cupping her, feeling her heat through the layers of clothing.

His mouth came down on hers and Melissa eagerly reached for him.

'You're driving me crazy,' she murmured when he lifted his mouth to trail hot kisses across her cheek, down to her throat.

'Then we're even, because you drive me crazy with wanting you whenever I look at you!' He moved his hand against her and she arched up to meet him, her eyes soft with love.

'Dad, Dad.' Max could be heard running in the hall.

'Dammit, he can't have eaten the cookies by now.' Bret sat up and pulled Melissa to a sitting position. Max burst into the nursery, his face beaming.

'Marta is bringing us all a tray. She has cookies and lemonade, because it's so warm.'

'That's wonderful. What a nice treat,' Melissa said, her voice brimming with laughter at Bret's frustrated look. She reached over and lightly touched his hand to let him know she was sorry it had ended as well. Why had he picked this time to kiss her? Why not come to her bed at night when they would not be disturbed?

That night they went to the dinner party given by one of Bret's friends. Melissa enjoyed herself and learned a bit more about the man she'd married. But when they came home he bade her a calm goodnight and remained downstairs when she went to bed. After the encounter in the nursery she'd expected him to join her. But he did not. It was a long time before she slept.

On Sunday Bret surprised them all and took them to Schloss Hellbrunn, just south of the city. They dressed in casual clothes suitable for the hot day. Bret led them in, Melissa's hand firmly in his, Max running around exploring everything.

'Now this is known as the oldest formal garden in Austria. But the builder had a sense of humour. Watch out for water fountains.' They strolled down pathways, only to be surprised when from either side streams of water arched over the walkways, spraying everyone in the path.

Melissa laughed as she tried to outrun the water. Bret watched her, his eyes alight with amusement. Max wanted to see it done again, so they had to wait for the next time. It was erratic, and they never knew exactly when it would happen.

From there they wandered to the table that would spray diners, and even one fountain where the water came from the horns of the reindeer.

'This is fun!' Melissa said, dodging yet another spray. 'But I wouldn't want to come in winter.'

'In winter, we can ski at Innsbruck.'

She looked up, then away, catching her breath. Would she still be here in winter? The deal between the companies would be long finished by then. Would Bret let her stay after the deal was signed? Did he want her to stay?

'Now what?' he asked, turning her back to face him.

'Nothing. Where are we eating lunch? I draw the line at that table we saw earlier.'

He chuckled. 'No, we are going to a small farm not far from here to look at a dog.'

'Great. Won't Max be surprised?'

The puppy was a darling, and Max fell in love with him immediately. Melissa did, too. He was of mixed parentage, tan with a white chest and white paws. The mother was not particularly big, so he would grow to be the right size for the house and for Max.

On the ride home, Melissa asked how Bret had learned about the farm. 'Are they friends of yours?'

'No, my secretary recommended them when I mentioned you thought Max should have a puppy.'

'A good choice, I think,' she murmured, looking again at the happy boy in the back, hugging his new puppy. She looked back at Bret, pleased that he'd taken up her suggestion of a puppy. Wished wistfully that he'd listen to her on other matters as well. But if the plan she and Gerry worked on was successful, he'd soon know she was not a thief.

The day as a family had been fun. Melissa hoped they would do more things like that. She remembered doing things with her father and mother when she was small—going sightseeing around London, visiting the beach. Once they'd taken a week-long trip to Scotland.

True to his word, the next week Bret deposited an enormous sum of money into Melissa's bank account. When she protested, he turned aside her objections and said only that he would provide for his wife, and told her not to argue.

Bret began to stay away from home more and more. He would skip dinner, working so he explained it. Yet he was always available for social outings, and Melissa began to wish for more parties to attend so that she could at least spend some time with Bret, even in the company of others.

When he was home, he seemed tired, distracted, and busy. Several nights when she went upstairs to bed he'd still be at his desk in his study, reviewing papers, jotting notes.

Max was back in school, so Melissa was at a loose end during the greater part of the day. She wrote to her mother and brought her up to date on all the news, keeping some of it back so as not to worry her, and thanked her for coming to Melissa's rescue, even though she had not needed the money after all.

But she needed to do more. Marta and other staff kept the house immaculate. Max was only home in the afternoons and evenings and Melissa just didn't have enough to keep her busy.

Would Bret stand for her getting a job? She wanted to broach the subject with him but never found the right moment. Gerry was keeping her informed on the negotiations with Larbard Industries. But time was running out. If they didn't plant the false proposal soon, the real one would be sent and they'd lose their chance to catch the person delaying the deal. She couldn't leave it like that.

She rose early the next morning and was already at breakfast when Bret came in. He raised his eyebrows on seeing her.

'Good morning.'

'Good morning. I wanted to catch you for a ride into Salzburg,' she said.

'Shopping?' he asked, taking his seat and reaching for the coffee she poured him.

'Yes. My mother's birthday is in a couple of weeks. I wanted to get something to send to her.' And look for a job. But that she'd tell him when she had found one. He might be angry, but she'd faced his anger before.

'Have lunch with me,' he invited.

'I'd like that,' she said shyly.

Melissa found some wooden carvings, representative of the area, for her mother. She arranged to have them shipped from the little shop. Then she went to the British Consulate. She discussed the possibility of her working as an English tutor with the nice man referred to her. He said there were always enquiries about people to help tutor and he'd be back in touch in a few days with some people she could contact.

Satisfied that things were working out, Melissa headed for Bret's office in a happy frame of mind.

He had not objected to her meeting him there, and had told her to call up from the lobby when she arrived. Instead she took the lift to the top floor and stepped out. Immediately she was taken back several weeks. To the time Mr Millan had first led his coterie to the conference-room. She smiled sadly; so much had changed for her since then, and she'd never had the slightest premonition.

She nodded to the receptionist and told her she would find Bret. The girl smiled in recognition.

'You know where the office is, Frau Terrell. Have a nice lunch.'

As she walked down the empty hall, Melissa peeked into the conference-room and caught Gerry's eye. He rose and hurried out to meet her, his smile of welcome a balm to her nerves.

'Trying it out?' he asked softly, following her into the hall, glancing around to make sure they were alone.

She giggled and shook her head. 'I'm just meeting Bret for lunch. But it's going to be harder than I thought. I'll have to get off on another floor and sneak up the stairs. You'll have to unlock the stairwell door.'

'We'll set it up by phone and then I'll unlock it in the late afternoon. If I can't reach you that day, I won't tell the others about the proposal being here.'

'How much longer, do you think?'

'Maybe three more days. We lost another set of reports last night. But we're almost finished. Why does Bret pick now to stay home?'

'Because he wants to spend time with his wife, perhaps?' Bret's voice penetrated like a lance.

Melissa looked around; he'd come out of his office and approached them without their being aware of him.

'Hi.' Her smile was shaky. How much had he heard?

'Did you wish to spend time with my wife?' His voice was hard, his face ruthless.

Gerry shook his head. 'Just saying hello since she walked by. Be seeing you.' He nodded and quickly returned to the conference-room.

Melissa turned back to Bret, her heart dropping. Now what did he think?

'In future, do not come to this office. Do not have anything to do with Gerry Toliver, is that clear?'

Melissa shivered at Bret's icy tone. She knew how hard he could be; she'd experienced his implacable anger when he'd thought she'd taken the folders. She nodded. There was nothing else to be said. She couldn't tell him what she was really trying to do.

CHAPTER ELEVEN

LUNCH was a disaster. Melissa counted the minutes until it was over. Bret ate and spoke only when addressed directly. She didn't know why he'd bothered. She was glad to escape and return home when the meal was over.

That night, Bret was late returning home. He shut himself up in the study when he did arrive, and closed the door, clearly letting Melissa know that he didn't wish to see her.

The next morning Gerry called.

'He's gone.'

'Who?' Melissa asked.

'Terrell. He's gone to Innsbruck for two days. I'll let everyone know about the proposal today. Can you get in?'

'Yes. I'll be there no later than four. How will I know the proposal?'

'I'll put it in a bright yellow folder. It's close to what I think will be the final plan, but not the real thing.'

'That's good. Wish me luck.'

'You know it, Melissa. I wish I could stay.'

'No, we've been through that. I'll be fine; I just want to know who's doing it. I won't try to stop them.'

Melissa hung up the phone, already keyed up in anticipation of the evening's work. She would find out at last who had set her up. Find out and then tell Bret. He had to know that she had not betrayed him.

The day dragged by. Melissa carefully told Marta that she was going to an early dinner with friends, then worried that she wouldn't be able to get out of the house in the dark jeans and jersey she was planning to wear. It was much too casual for a dinner.

But luck was on her side. When she called a cab, Marta was in with Max and Melissa escaped them both.

The cab deposited her a couple of blocks from Austerling Ltd. Melissa didn't want someone seeing her from one of the windows and wondering what she was doing. Her hair was pulled back in a French braid, and she'd thought about using blacking on her face. But she'd known she was getting giddy with nerves when she'd had that thought.

She reached the ladies' room with no one seeing her. She locked a cubicle and sat down, keeping her feet from the floor. Time dragged. She should have brought a book to read, or something. Checking her watch for the hundredth time, she saw that only five minutes had passed since the last time. Everyone would not have left yet.

Gerry was waiting until after everyone had left before leaving himself. Or leaving with the last of the Austerling group. That had been their plan. Surely the person would not come back before the cleaners were finished. They could be witnesses. Melissa was counting on the person coming back late tonight.

When she heard the cleaners, she left the ladies' room and hurried back to the stairs, holding the door slightly ajar so as not to be locked on the landing. When they left, she'd go to the ante-room and wait.

At last the place was quiet. Quiet and dark. Slowly she eased open the door, listening intently. She heard nothing. Slipping into the office floor, she let the door close behind her with a soft click. She started down the hall, then turned right past the bank of files. Past the door to Bret's office. Down the hall to the conference-room. The door was open but it was too dark to see the furniture. Sliding along the wall, she came to the opening of the antechamber. She stepped inside.

Immediately a bright light flashed in her face. Melissa was blinded by the glare and threw her hands before her eyes to shelter them from the light.

'What the hell are you doing here?'

Her heart sank. It was Bret.

'I can explain,' she said, but would he listen?

'I'm sure you can. You learned today that the proposal had come in, didn't you? You came to get it, is that it?'

'Shh. Bret, shine the light somewhere else. You're blinding me.'

It snapped off. His hard hand jerked her up against his body, slamming her into his hard chest as his fingers bit into the soft flesh of her arms.

'I could kill you for this, Melissa.' His voice was deadly, cold. 'I had doubts, but this confirms everything.'

'Bret, listen to me for a minute. It's not what you think.' She whispered, still hoping the real culprit would arrive. 'Gerry and I rigged this. That's not the real proposal. We're trying to find out who is sabotaging the negotiations, who planted those files in my case.'

'Good try, my dear. Good comeback. But I don't believe you. For a while I tried; I watched what was going on in case what you'd said had been the truth. But nothing happened. With you gone, things settled down.'

'Not true. Gerry has a list of incidents.'

'Is he your accomplice?'

'Damn you, Bret, listen to me,' she hissed.

One hand covered her mouth and his other arm drew her against him tightly, so that Melissa couldn't move.

'Hush,' he hissed in her ear. 'I heard something.'

The seconds dragged by as she was held tightly against her husband's chest, his hand relaxing from her mouth, slowly moving away when he was sure she'd keep quiet. Melissa closed her eyes to hear better, but only heard the soft, steady beat of Bret's heart, the soft whisper of his breath.

Then she heard a footstep. Instantly she drew up, turned towards the door to the conference-room.

Bret pushed her behind him and moved to the edge of the door, his eyes watching the conference-room.

A light appeared, aimed on the table. Picking up the distinctive yellow folder, it stopped roaming. Melissa strained to see who it was. She stepped out, but Bret hauled her behind him again, his hand tight on her arm. He was waiting to see more.

And was rewarded. A hand withdrew a page from the folder, crumpling it up and putting it in a pocket. Soon another page was withdrawn, crumpled. The folder was tossed back on the table. But before the person could leave Bret switched on his powerful light, shining it on the startled face of Karl Müller.

Melissa gave a short gasp, staring in shock at one of her husband's trusted managers.

'Melissa, go to the phone in my office and call the building security. The number is beside the phone. Be quick.'

She stepped around Bret and hurried to his office, flipping on the lights as she went. In only moments she'd returned to the conference-room.

Bret must have asked Karl why he'd done it, because he was talking rapidly, trying to explain what happened, excuse his behaviour.

'. . .depleted the stock even more. I've been here my entire working life. I wanted stock in the firm. But you keep selling it off. The German deal ended up a disaster; you knew that at the time. I was to get some stock from that deal, but it fell through.'

'You helped Louisa?'

'She couldn't do it by herself,' Karl said scornfully. He looked at Melissa when she entered, his face almost a sneer. 'I thought to stop this one, but didn't know how far off I was with the relationship between you two. Instead of sending the London company packing, you married her.'

'So you put the folders in my briefcase.' She wanted no room for error on this. Bret had to know, though he must guess now that she had not taken the folders.

'Of course.' He sank down on one of the chairs, suddenly ageing. He stared at the folders on the table, his hand moving to the crumpled pages in his pocket. There was no getting away from the act tonight.

In only a moment, the uniformed security guard who had stopped Melissa so many weeks ago appeared, took in the situation and stepped over to Karl Müller. 'If you'll come with me, sir.'

'I'll want to press charges if I can,' Bret said to the guard. 'Make sure he never sets foot on this floor again.'

Bret said nothing about the revelation as he walked quietly along beside Melissa, leading her to the car. She was keyed up with the final vindication, yet curiously apprehensive. Bret was not saying anything. Yet the silence was almost deafening. There was no reason for her to remain in Austria. Bret now knew she had not been the one to interfere with the sale. Why didn't he say something? She wished she knew what he was thinking.

He opened the door to the BMW and helped her in, slamming it after her and moving to get in behind the wheel. Turning to her, he surveyed her in the dim street-light.

'I owe you an apology, Melissa. I'm sorry I didn't believe you when you first told me you hadn't taken the files. But I thought the evidence overwhelmingly proved you had,' he said stiffly, his eyes meeting hers at last. He seemed somehow distant, more formal than she had ever seen him.

'I'm just glad it's finally cleared up. It's quite awful when you continue to tell the truth and no one believes you.' Actually the people who knew her had known she would never do such a thing. But Bret had been the one who counted most. And he had not believed her.

'It was totally inexcusable on my part and I apologise.'

She reached across and touched one of his hands. He jerked back as if she'd burned him. She looked away, trying to hide the hurt she felt at his reaction to her touch.

'You were there tonight. Why? You could be expected to think that I was trying to sabotage the deal, after your experience with Louisa,' she said gently. Was she never to please this man?

'You're nothing like Louisa, as you have proved over and over. But I was too blind to see. Too afraid to trust my own judgement. Did you know it was Karl all along?'

'No. Although actually we had it narrowed down to him or Erich. They were the only ones who I thought would know the details of the German deal and the ramifications. And have the opportunity to put the files in my briefcase.'

'We?'

'Gerry Toliver and I. He was helping me find out what was going on. He knew I wouldn't take the folders. But he couldn't discover who had.'

'I would have trusted Karl for anything. I never knew he wanted shares in the company, though he's been here since long before I started.'

'Why were you there tonight, Bret? Gerry said you were going to Innsbruck.'

He was silent, staring out over the quiet street, lost in thought. 'I do have to go to Innsbruck, had planned to leave this afternoon. But when I heard from my secretary that Gerry was telling everyone that the final proposal was in, I postponed my trip. I wanted to see if anyone would come back tonight to take it, or change it.'

Melissa's heart took wing. 'Why?'

'I guess I wasn't convinced you'd taken the files.'

'You sounded convinced.'

'That was when I first discovered them. But over the weeks you've shown you aren't the mercenary woman that Louisa was. You refused the necklace, though it's worth a lot of money. And you didn't badger me for funds, but spent your own money. Even called your mother for more rather than ask me. I wondered about you. I began to pay closer attention to the negotiations, to the day-to-day happenings. I didn't have Gerry's list, though. And when I found you there tonight, I thought it was proof positive that you were the one behind everything.'

'Like Louisa.'

'Damn it, Melissa, I've told you before, you're nothing like Louisa!' He was silent for a long moment, staring out at the empty street. 'You've kept your end of the bargain and I'll keep mine. You're free to return to England as soon as you want.'

She stared at him in shock, her heart dropping. She really hadn't expected him to say that.

'Max has the puppy now, and is back in school. It won't be so hard on him,' Bret added.

What about me? she wanted to shout. What about how hard it will be *for me*? But she said nothing, merely nodded, afraid her voice would give her away.

'It's time I got back to work. I was growing bored at home all day with Max in school,' she said in a brittle tone, wondering how she was going to bear it in the years ahead.

'I still have to go to Innsbruck on business tomorrow. I'll be back in the afternoon. Can you hold your departure until after then? I'll take you to the airport.'

'Sure.' Tears threatened and Melissa held them back with monumental effort. 'Can we go home now?' She wanted to gain the privacy of her room to give way to the tears and heartache that threatened to overwhelm her.

'Very well.' He turned, studying her, cupping her cheek with his warm hand, his thumb brushing lightly across her lips.

'I'm sorry I didn't believe you, Melissa. It would have made everything different.' He lowered his face and kissed her gently, softly, briefly.

Melissa sat in stunned silence as he drove swiftly through the city streets, traffic non-existent so late. All too soon they reached the road to Bret's house. Arriving home, she entered the silent house ahead of him, tears now starting, flowing down her cheeks. *Home*, but only for a few more hours. Then she'd be gone. Slowly she climbed the stairs, touching the railing in a loving caress, trying to see the old house through tear-drenched eyes, but everything was blurred. Reaching her bed, she sank down against the soft pillows and gave way to the heartache that would forever be with her, muffling her sobs so he wouldn't hear. Would never suspect.

The next morning Melissa began packing. It shouldn't take her too long; she hadn't that many clothes. It was hard to think now that she had just come for a short business trip. She'd been here well over a month. So much had happened, but she couldn't think of all that now; there'd be time when she was back in England. Endless amounts of time. The things she'd brought were quickly packed. She left out one suit to wear home.

As she fingered the evening dresses she'd purchased since marrying Bret, she remembered the different times she'd worn them. This one to the concert, this one to the dinner party at the Wolfstaus', the off-the-shoulder blue one to the ballet. Should she even take them with her? She couldn't imagine wearing them again. They would forever remind her of Bret.

She wandered to the window. She would have liked to go to the meadow one more time. But it was raining. The wind blew strongly and she feared branches breaking in the forest surrounding the meadow. She sighed. She wished she could have gone one more time, ridden Schönfeld, marvelled at the view, felt the sun on her face, seen the colourful wild flowers brushed by the breeze, seen all of Salzburg spread out before her. But perhaps it was better this way. She had her memories.

It was still raining by the time Max came home from school, and growing cooler. He told her how the wind had shaken the car that delivered him home each day, and the rain almost made visibility impossible.

They lit the fire in the nursery and sat cosily inside

listening to the rain beat against the windows in a torrential fury. The wind was loud, whistling around the old stone house, through the tall pines and firs that swayed in its force. It grew dark earlier than normal because of the storm.

They ate their snacks before the fire, then went to play with the new puppy. The puppy was still banished to the kitchen until he was house-trained, so they visited him there. Marta complained good-naturedly but laughed at the puppy's antics with Max.

Throughout the day, Melissa was conscious of the clock ticking. Soon she'd be gone, no longer a part of this family. Her heart ached with the thought. How would she bear it with only memories to keep her company in her small apartment in London? She'd miss Max, and the puppy, and Marta. Bret. Most of all Bret.

Melissa tried to keep her sunny disposition, not wanting Max to know she was leaving. She'd let his father make that announcement. So she laughed and read to him and played soldiers, savouring the time she spent with him, storing up his cute comments to bring out in her memory in the future.

Maybe Bret would allow Max to visit her occasionally, if she asked him.

When the wind rattled the kitchen door, Melissa shivered, thinking of Bret having to drive in this weather. She hoped the storm wasn't as bad over Innsbruck as it was outside.

'Frau Terrell, there is a phone call, can you take it?' Marta appeared in the door of the nursery during the light supper Melissa was sharing with Max.

'Certainly. Is it Herr Terrell?' Maybe he was calling to say he would be delayed, was even staying in Innsbruck. She wouldn't expect him to drive home in such a storm. The rain still beat against the windows, the wind howling in the evening darkness.

'No, Frau, it is one of his employees.'

Melissa hurried down the hall to Bret's bedroom, knowing there was an extension in there. 'Hello?'

'Frau Terrell, is Herr Terrell at home? This is Erich Meyer.'

'No. He had to go to Innsbruck.' Didn't the people at his firm know where he was?'

'He left there some hours ago. I thought he would be home by now. He did not come to the office; I am still here. But I need some information to send a telex to America. Could you have him call me when he gets home? I'll wait here a little longer.'

'Yes. I'll tell him as soon as he gets here.' Melissa put down the receiver, apprehension building. She shook off her worry. Bret had certainly pulled off somewhere to wait for the worst of the storm to pass. He probably was sitting in a warm café somewhere sipping coffee and wondering how much longer the storm would last.

Then why didn't he call her? she asked herself.

Yet why should he think she would worry about him? The only time she'd tried to tell him she loved him he'd scoffed at her. He thought she was glad to be going back to England. Alone. How blind could he get?

She sat down on the edge of his bed, her hand brushing against the dark coverlet, feeling the softness of the bed beneath her. She looked around the room, at the old and heavy furniture. This was never her room; she'd never been asked to move in. Would it be easier or harder to leave if she had?

Sighing for what could not be, she rose and went to rejoin Max. This was probably their last night together, and she wanted to make the most of it. She wanted Max to think of her fondly in the years ahead, as she would remember him.

Melissa kept her worry about Bret at bay until Max had gone to sleep. It was after eight-thirty. Bret should have been home by now. Or had he gone to the office as Erich expected? She hurried down to the study and went to the phone. When she called the office, the phone rang and rang, but there was no answer. Had Bret arrived and given Erich the information he needed? Was he even now on his way home?

Marta had built a nice fire in the study. It gave warmth to the room despite the storm, but Melissa couldn't feel it. She stared at the flames for a long time, wondering where Bret was, worrying, the cold deep in her heart.

She left the study and went to the windows on either side of the heavy front door. Peering out, she could see nothing in the stygian darkness. But she could still hear the rain pounding down, the wail of the wind in the trees, around the eaves of the house. Shivering, she went back to the study. She'd wait a little longer; maybe he was even now driving up the hill towards their house.

When the clock chimed nine, she threw down the magazine she'd been trying to read and went to the phone again. There was still no answer at the office. Pulling the directory from the shelf, she thumbed through it until she found Erich's home phone number. She dialled with shaking fingers, afraid to hear what he might say.

'Have you heard from Bret?' she asked when he came on the line.

'No, Frau Terrell, he never came to the office. I finally sent the telex without the information.'

'You're sure he left Innsbruck?'

'Yes, we called there when we first wanted to send the telex. He left shortly after lunch.'

It was less than a three-hour drive. He should have been back ages ago. Where was he?

Melissa thanked him and said she would have Bret call Erich upon his return. She hung up the phone and sat staring at it, her heart pounding.

The knock at the door surprised her. Relief flooded through her body. She rose and walked swiftly to the heavy door. Had he forgotten his key? He would be soaked, the rain was coming down so hard.

She threw open the door, the smile of welcome fading as she saw the two strangers standing before her. They wore black waterproofs and the water ran down them like a waterfall. Their hats shielded their faces from the worst of the rain, but even so their cheeks gleamed in the light spilling from the entrance hall.

'Frau Terrell?' The older man spoke in German.

'Yes. Come in, it's pouring.' She stepped aside to let them in as fear clutched her heart. She recognised the insignia of the Salzburg police on their collars. Stalling to avoid whatever they could say, she closed the door.

'It's a terrible storm,' she said inanely, speaking to them in German.

'Frau Terrell, is your husband home?'

'No.' She swallowed hard. 'He had to go to Innsbruck today.' Why were they here? She was afraid to ask.

The two men exchanged glances. The first then pulled a small notebook from his pocket and flipped it open.

'Does Herr Terrell own a black BMW, registration plates. . .?'

Melissa couldn't hear through the roaring in her ears. She stepped back, blindly seeking the chair that stood near the door. She sank in it, her eyes fixed upon the policeman. He had stopped speaking and was looking at her.

'Bret owns a black BMW; I don't know the registration plates. We haven't been married very long.' As if that explained everything.

The older man looked pained.

'I'm sorry, Frau Terrell.' His voice was soft, sorrowful. 'The car was found, smashed rather badly, I'm sorry to say, on a dangerous section of highway between here and Innsbruck. There is a cliff, a sharp turn.' He shrugged. 'We did not find your husband, madam, but there was blood in the car. Have you heard anything?'

'No.' Panic welled. Bret had to be all right. She couldn't bear it if anything happened to Bret. 'He was expected back a long time ago. But no one has heard from him. I was just in touch with one of his employees.'

God, it was awful. Was he all right? What if he was injured, or worse? How could she stand living if Bret was gone forever?

'It may be that he is fine, madam. But maybe he has wandered away injured, even fallen further down the cliff. We are looking for him.'

She closed her eyes and nodded. But if he had wandered away in this awful storm, did he have a chance? He'd die of exposure before the night was over. Especially if he was injured. She couldn't stand it!

She stood up, glancing around her. There must be something she could do.

'Madam, we are doing all that can be done. If you

hear from him, please let us know. We will continue to look for him.' The man's eyes were sympathetic. As were the second man's.

Melissa nodded and tried to smile, but she couldn't. 'If I hear I'll call. You'll let me know instantly if you find him?' *When* you find him, she amended silently.

'Yes, Frau Terrell. You will be all right?'

'Yes. I'll wait here. His. . .our. . .son is upstairs. I'll wait with him.'

It was the first time she'd really thought of Max as her son. If something happened to Bret, he'd be her responsibility.

But nothing would happen to Bret. He had to be all right. *He had to!*

The house seemed big and empty and lonely when the police officers departed. Yet despite the vastness of the house the sound and fury of the storm was still heard. Bret couldn't be out in it. It was awful.

She walked back to the study; the warm glow of the lamps there seemed friendlier than the harsh light in the entrance hall. She could imagine Bret at his desk, standing at the window. A lot had happened in this room. She'd give anything to have him here again.

Melissa sank down, staring out of the dark rain-splattered windows. Her mind was numb. She couldn't think of him as gone. He'd be back soon. She had to believe that.

And maybe she had to think of what she was going to do when he did return. She couldn't leave. God, she couldn't bear it. She loved him. They'd had some happy times together. She thought about the afternoons playing with Max, their trip to the Schloss Hellbrunn, the concerts and dinner parties, and the rides through peaceful meadows. His kisses inflamed

her. Their wedding night had been special, wonderful.
And he still wanted her. She knew that.

Her face warmed. She remembered every time he'd
kissed her, touched her. The only night they'd made
love. He shouldn't have done that if he wanted an
annulment. Yet he had, and told her there'd be no
annulment.

He had to be all right!

Restless, she got up and walked around the room,
wishing there were something else that could be done.
Hoping he was all right, had found shelter, was not
injured badly. She walked out into the entrance hall,
staring at the door as if it would open and admit Bret.
But she heard only the rain, saw only the puddles the
policemen had caused from their dripping waterproofs.
She probably should wipe it up.

Instead she walked slowly up the stairs, moving down
the hall to Max's room. The light from the hall enabled
her to see him, peacefully sleeping, his cheeks rosy, his
blond hair tousled a little from sleep. She smiled as
tears welled. He was so precious, she couldn't tell him
something had happened to his daddy. He'd already
lost his mother; he couldn't lose his father, too.

Melissa couldn't stand the waiting. She went back to
her room and stood by the window. Dared she trust
her instincts? Or would she set herself up for heartbreak? She turned and picked up her suitcase. Carrying
it down the hall, she boldly entered Bret's room and
plopped it on the bed. Unpacking everything, she
found room for her clothes in his wardrobe, in one of
the cavernous drawers of the large tallboy.

Making two or three trips back and fourth, she soon
had all her evening dresses and her things from the
bathroom in place. She sat on his bed and looked

around her. Tears threatened again. What if she'd left it too late? What if he never returned?

The sweep of headlights arced through the window. Melissa raised her head. Had the police returned? Had they heard something? She rose slowly and started down the hall almost in a trance.

CHAPTER TWELVE

MELISSA heard the click of the lock without really registering what it was. Then she heard the door open and hope burgeoned.

'Bret?'

She reached the top of the stairs just as he entered and closed the door behind him.

'Bret,' she said softly, starting down the stairs, running down them lightly, her eyes only for him.

'Bret. Bret! *Bret!*' Each time his name was louder until she almost shouted with joy.

He looked up as she ran down the stairs and stared at her, wonder and something else dawning in his eyes. Her hair was swirling around her face. The warm woollen trousers displayed the womanly shape of her hips and her long legs, her soft sweater outlined her rounded breasts. He took a deep breath at the sight of her and opened his arms as she launched herself at him.

Melissa wound her arms tightly around his neck, hugging him as close as she could, never wanting to let him go. She'd been so afraid, and now he was here. He had come back and she didn't want to let him go. Ever.

His arms held her, and Bret sagged back against the closed door, wondering what he'd done to receive such a gift, not questioning it at all. He just held Melissa, letting his body feel hers along his length.

'Oh, God, Bret, I was so afraid. I thought you were dead. The police couldn't find you and Erich hadn't heard from you and you didn't call here and the storm is awful.' She gave a gulp that was suspiciously like a sob and hugged him even harder.

'Melissa, sweetheart, I'm fine.' His hands branded her back as he held her tightly.

'The police were here, Bret. They said the car was smashed and there was blood.' She leaned back in his arms slightly to study him. Ther was a white bandage securely afffixed to his forehead. He looked tired, drained. She saw flecks of blood on his coat. And felt the dampness.

'Bret, you're soaking wet!'

'I got wet earlier, but almost dried in the hospital.' He looked down at her distressed face and lowered his mouth to hers.

Melissa closed her eyes, at peace at last. He was safe and as his mouth claimed hers she gave him all the love she had. His kiss was all the sweeter for the fear she'd gone through the last few hours.

When he shivered she pulled back. 'Bret, you need to get out of these wet clothes. Take a hot shower and get into dry, warm things. Are you really all right?' Her eyes searched every wonderful feature, trying to convince herself he was safe, home and safe.

'Yes, I'm really all right. Come up with me,' he said, his voice husky. She nodded, her eyes never leaving his. The blue of his deepened and he leaned over to brush his lips against hers. Taking her hand, he started to climb the stairs.

'What happened?' she asked as he used the railing to assist him up the steps.

'Banged my head pretty badly, and got soaked, but other than that I'm fine. The car's a wreck, though. Lucky it didn't slide down the embankment. Got caught against a tree.'

She shivered, picturing the wreck in her mind.

'The storm?' she asked.

'Yes. The roads were awful, slick, even flooded in some areas. Tree limbs and branches were being blown down across the pavement. I swerved to avoid a large one, skidded across the wet asphalt and slid off the shoulder and slammed into the tree.'

He pushed open the door to his bedroom, his hand tight around Melissa's as if he thought she wouldn't come with him.

She had a moment's hesitation. She hadn't explained to him that she'd moved into his room. Would he find that presumptuous?

He pulled her inside and shut the door behind her. Melissa glanced around, but there was nothing to show she'd moved her things in. Until he went into the bathroom. She grew nervous. How would be react? Maybe she should say something.

Glancing up at him, she smiled tremulously. Her heart melted when she looked at him. His hair was honey-coloured from the rain, his eyes the deep blue she loved. The white bandage contrasted sharply against his tan.

'Stitches?' she asked as she stared at the bandage, trying not to envisage the accident. She'd been so scared.

'Yes, seven. I'll be fine—another scar, though. A nice older couple found me by the side of the road in the pouring rain and gave me a lift to Salzburg to the hospital. Because of the storm it was a while before they could look at me. It's not critical, you know, and there were many accidents because of the storm. They had to take the critical ones first, of course.'

He shrugged off his damp coat and then held it a moment, as if he didn't know what to do with it.

Melissa reached out and took it. 'We can put your

clothes in the bathroom. The suit is probably ruined, but we'll worry about that later.'

He nodded and undid the buttons on his shirt, shivering a little again.

'You need a hot bath,' she said, moving towards the bathroom.

'No, a shower will do me. God, I'm tired.'

'And achy, too, I bet.' She turned on the shower and adjusted the heat. Stepping back, she bumped into Bret. He'd taken off his shirt and his shoulder gleamed in the light, his chest was wide and solid, and it was all Melissa could do not to push up against him so that she could feel his strength again.

'Wait for me,' he ordered as she stepped around him, breathless with wanting him.

She nodded and pulled the door shut behind her. She walked to the window, and gave thanks that he'd come back safely. The phone rang and she turned to answer it. It was the police, notifying her that her husband had been located, he had been treated at the hospital and would soon be home. She thanked them for letting her know, smiling at their slowness. She quickly called Erich to let him know Bret was home and was all right. Then she sat down on the bed, Indian fashion, to wait for Bret. How would he react to her moving into his room?

When the shower stopped, her heartbeat increased. Soon he'd come out and she'd have to tell him she loved him and didn't want to return to England. He had to let her stay. The experience of this night proved to her that she needed to be with him. Needed to know he was safe and well. And maybe they could find some happiness together. With Max.

Bret opened the door and stepped into the bedroom. He glanced a moment at Melissa and then moved to the tallboy along the wall. She stared at him. He had a towel wrapped low around his hips. And that was all. His back was sculpted, his muscles clearly defined and taut. She longed to run her hands over him.

He pulled open the drawer that had her lingerie in it. It shared the space with his briefs. He was still for a long moment. Melissa held her breath. What would he say? She stared at his back, trying to read his mind, her nerves stretching. After a long moment, he moved and withdrew a pair of cotton briefs.

He dropped his towel and Melissa felt a wave of heat and desire wash through her. His buttocks were firm and tight and she watched the play of muscles as he stepped into his briefs and pulled them up. Her breasts ached for his touch, her stomach was full of butterflies and overwhelming longing for him built up deep within her.

He yanked open another drawer and withdrew an old sweatshirt. Pulling it on he walked to the wardrobe and opened the door, again standing still for a long moment as he saw Melissa's dresses hanging near his suits.

Why didn't he say something? Anything?

He took out a pair of jeans and pulled them on, turning to stare at her assessingly as his hands slowly pulled up the zip.

She tried to smile, tried to be sophisticated and worldly. But her heart was beating too hard and she was so afraid he might ask her to leave. Her eyes never left his, her uncertainty clear. Why didn't he say something? What was he thinking?

His eyes still on her, he walked over to the edge of the bed and stared down at her.

'These are warm clothes, but maybe I don't need

them. Maybe I'll have something else to warm me tonight,' he said, easing down on the bed beside her.

She cleared her throat. 'Did the shower warm you up?'

'Yes.'

She dropped her gaze to her hands, which were surreptitiously trying to wipe the dampness away on her trouser legs; it was safer to stare there than into Bret's eyes.

'I like it better when you wear shorts and skimpy tops,' he said, lying back, taking one of her hands in his. He played with her fingers as he lay there for a long moment, his eyes closed.

Melissa could tell he was tired. His head probably ached. He should go to sleep.

'So, do you want to tell me what your things are doing in my bathroom, and what your clothes are doing in my drawers and wardrobe?' he asked after a moment, his hands idly playing with hers, his eyes still closed.

'I—er—I thought maybe I wouldn't go back to England.'

'Why's that?' His voice gave nothing away.

Melissa stared at him. How did he feel about this change? She hadn't a clue.

'I thought I'd stay here.'

'And I thought you were bored here.'

'I have a job.'

He opened his eye a slit and stared at her. His voice noticeably harder, he asked, 'Doing what?'

'Tutoring English.'

'And that would be enough?' He relaxed.

'Yes.' Until the babies came, she thought, wondering if she and Bret would ever have babies together.

Wanting one from him. Another adorable boy like Max, or maybe a little girl. Or both.

He tugged her hand and she toppled over, lying on her side by him. Straightening her legs, she let herself lean against him, shifting hands so that she propped her head up on one and let the other find his fingers and twine with them on his chest.

They lay like that for a long time. Melissa wondered if he was falling asleep.

'I love you,' he said softly.

Her heart lurched, then pounded in her chest as incredible happiness spread through her. Jason had been right!

'Oh, Bret, I love you too. I think I always have. But you insisted it was only lust.'

He opened his eyes to look at her and pulled her across him, to lie cradled across his chest. His arms held her tightly, one hand threaded through the soft waves of her chestnut hair, massaging her neck, combing the silky strands.

'I was wrong about that as well as other things. I was a bloody fool. God, who would have thought Karl would do such a thing? I should never have doubted you. But even when I did I wanted you.' His voice was harsh with self-recrimination.

'Even then?' she said softly, snuggling closer. 'I think I've loved you since I met you in the meadow. That's why I went back on that Sunday.'

'And I was glad you did. I wanted to see you again and had no way to find you.'

'Until I showed up at your work.'

'But I didn't know that on the weekend.' He was silent for a long moment, feeling her soft femininity warm his soul. 'Why did you change your mind about staying, Melissa?'

'I was planning to go to England. I thought that was what you wanted.' She felt him tense up beneath her and she reached up and gave him a soft kiss at the side of his mouth, smiling in delight as his chiselled lips softened into a slight smile. His eyes remained closed and she snuggled up against him again, feeling safe and warm and loved.

'I even packed today. But when you didn't come home, and then the police came and said you might be injured or worse, I knew I couldn't leave. I just couldn't, Bret. I love you too much. So I decided to stay. Here.'

'That love shines through in everything you do, sweetheart. In your interest in Max, in your putting up with a pig of a husband who wouldn't even believe you when you told the truth. . .'

'Hush, you can't talk about my husband like that,' she said firmly. 'Knowing your history with Louisa, I can understand why you had trouble believing me. Especially with the folders in my briefcase. Yet yesterday you gave me the benefit of the doubt. You were at the office last night as well as me. Though I admit I had thought to get more from you than a stiff apology and an order to return to England practically within hours, however.'

'God, sweetheart, I felt like the worst bastard in the world for having doubted you. I never thought you'd forgive me, want to stay. I wanted to see you once again after my trip to Innsbruck. I couldn't bear the thought of your leaving immediately, yet didn't think I could ask you to stay.'

His hand slipped beneath the edge of her sweater, his fingers tracing paths of icy fire along her back, up her spine. He unsnapped her bra and moved around to the soft swell of one breast, cupping it gently, taking its soft weight. Melissa was fast losing her mind.

'And I have to be grateful to Gerry Toliver, dammit,' he said.

She moved closer, savouring the feel of his hand against her, slowly building to the fiery delight she knew was coming. 'Why?' she mumbled, surprised she could still talk with his hands on her like that. Why did he bring up Gerry's name now?

'I was jealous of the two of you. Every time I saw you together I got mad. And yet he helped expose Karl. Damn!'

She giggled softly, moving her hand against his chest, laying her head against his shoulder and shifting slightly to give his hand better access.

'He's just a friend, and wanted to help me.'

'I can't return to England for a few more years, though I'm working on moving the company head-quarters there. The deal with Larbard will go a long way towards accomplishing that. But until then we're stuck in Salzburg,' he said, his hand softly insistent.

'I'm not leaving. Wherever you are is where I want to be,' she whispered, raising her mouth for a kiss.

'Tomorrow will you take the necklace I bought you? I wanted for you to have it, sweetheart. There are no strings attached to it. And while we're at it we'll go see Franz, too.'

'Herr Rollard? What for?'

'To tear up that damned pre-nuptial agreement, of course. It was a damnable idea to begin with. I said it before, you are nothing like Louisa. You are my wife, my love. I want to share everything I have with you. And if I should die before you, I'll leave you all my worldly goods.' He rolled her over on to her back, pushing up the soft sweater, exposing her breasts to his gaze.

'I don't care about all that, I only want your love, Bret,' she said as the dizzying delights of his touch on her breasts, the pull of longing and desire, began to spread. Her hands felt his strength beneath the warm sweatshirt. She thought her heart would burst with happiness.

'That you have, my darling. Actually you shall have it all. I love you more than anything in this world. I thought I loved Louisa at the beginning, but what I feel for you is much stronger, much deeper than anything I've felt before. I thought I'd ruined my only chance because I doubted you.'

'No, I love you too much, Bret. I won't leave unless you send me away.'

'That'll never happen. You're my heart and soul, the joy of this family. I love you, Melissa Terrell, for always!'

His mouth claimed hers in a searing kiss and the heat they built up between them removed the last vestige of cold and doubt from their lives for ever.

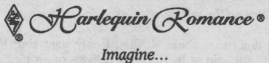

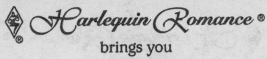
Harlequin Romance ®
brings you

Some men are worth waiting for!

Every month for a whole year Harlequin Romance will be bringing you some of the world's most eligible men in our special **Holding Out for a Hero** miniseries. They're handsome, they're charming but, best of all, they're single! Twelve lucky women are about to discover that finding Mr. Right is not a problem—it's holding on to him!

Watch for:

#3419 *KIT AND THE COWBOY*
by Rebecca Winters
Utah Writer of the Year

Available wherever Harlequin books are sold.

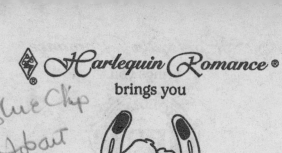

Harlequin Romance ®

brings you

How the West Was Wooed!

We've rounded up twelve of our most popular authors and the result is a whole year of romance, Western style. Every month we'll be bringing you a spirited, independent woman whose heart is about to be lassoed by a rugged, handsome, one-hundred-percent cowboy! Watch for...

- August: *TEMPORARY TEXAN*—Heather Allison

- September: *SOMETHING OLD, SOMETHING NEW*— Catherine Leigh

- October: *WYOMING WEDDING*—Barbara McMahon

- November: *THE COWBOY WANTS A WIFE!*— Susan Fox

Available wherever Harlequin books are sold.

HITCH-7